Intersection Thirteen

Intersection Thirteen

Matthew Buscemi

Published by Matthew Buscemi, 2021
Seattle, Washington USA

ISBN 978-1-62802-028-1

Typeset by Matthew Buscemi in MADE Evolve with Millard display

Just look at these superfluous creatures! They steal the creations of inventors and the treasures of the wise: culture they call their thievery—and for them it all turns to sickness and misfortune!

Just look at these superfluous creatures! Sick are they always; they vomit up their bile and call it a newspaper. They devour one another and cannot even digest themselves.

Just look at these superfluous creatures! Riches they acquire and become poorer by them. Power they desire, particularly the crowbar of power, money—these despicable creatures!

Look at them scramble, these swift little apes! They clamber over one another and thereby drag themselves into the dreck and the depths.

They all desire the throne: it is their madness,—as if happiness were to sit on a throne! Often it is dreck that sits on a throne—and often the throne itself sits on dreck.

...

There where the state ends, only there does the human being begin, the one who is not superfluous: there begins the song of the one who is necessary, the unique and irreplaceable sage.

from "On the New Idols," First Part, *Thus Spoke Zarathustra*
Friedrich Nietzsche

-32

Dear Arn,

I'm cutting this expedition off early. I've spent the last seven hours evading Hegemony scans. It's gotten so bad the last few days that I've decided to duck into a substratum where I'm hoping they won't follow me.

They hit Glezith's digital library with an EMP. I didn't think this would happen so soon, but here we are. At first I wasn't willing to believe it was the Hegemony, but then I checked my computer and they hadn't even bothered to stifle their quantum disruptions on entry.

The looks on the librarians' faces... I'm never going to forget that. And all because I was there. I was only just able to get out before they found the Liberalis.

I was able to save almost everything they had available publicly, I think. So, maybe someday we'll be able to go there and give it back to them. It's the least we could do. I didn't have time to get around to the private collectors. I'm hoping that my departure drew the Hegemony away and they won't want to make any more trouble for a defenseless world.

The Liberalis's computer is about two-thirds through what I got from them. Only about eleven percent correlation so far (up from ten yesterday), but that's something. None of the other worlds I've visited have yielded anything as good as that. A few scattered books here and there. No significant correlation from anything else.

The expedition as a whole has been mostly just long days of running from the Hegemony. My scans picked up a few other candidate worlds, but there was no way to slip into them without the Hegemony noticing. I've logged the worlds' coordinates so we can try again later.

The Liberalis is holding up well. He needs a good rinse down when he gets back. I haven't had enough of a break from Hegemony-watch in the last three weeks to clean either me or him. I'm sure we both reek. But his metaxic engines are in good shape. You should tell Zekk that I clocked a hegemony ship going 5.4 kdph a few days ago. If they keep improving their engines at that rate, we won't be able to outrun them for much longer.

As long as I don't pick up any more Hegemony ships in this substratum, I'll stick around for another day so I can complete a sweep. I know it's a long shot, but socially complex worlds have been discovered in substrata before.

I can't wait to see you when I get back.

All my love,
Mira

Mira hit the button that would initiate the encryption process and then fire her letter off through the metaxia toward its target. She leaned back in her chair, all the way back.

"Aurie," she said.

"What can I do for you?" the Liberalis's computer replied via the bridge speakers.

"Display scan progress."

A holographic image appeared above her reclined helm chair, a network of four hundred and seventy-two parallel Earths, about half of which had been dimmed out to light gray, meaning no human culture present, or, if present, none that had progressed past the writing stage. Four of the pinpoints of light shone bright blue and oscillated in intensity, indicating the worlds that Aurie was actively scanning. As Mira watched, one of the bright blue lights faded to gray, and a new light turned from white to blue.

"Any comm traffic?"

"None."

"Any Hegemony signals?"

"None."

"That's one bit of good news," Mira mumbled.

She looked around her bridge. Empty ration packs had piled up in one corner, clothes that had grown too sweat-stained to bearably wear in another. The comm panels were grimy, and some kind of mold or mildew had taken up residence in the corner of the ceiling next to the holographic emitters. It was all her own biological effluvia, she reminded herself. There hadn't been another living being in this room since she had left Earth.

A bright orange light caught her eye, and her attention shot back to the holographic display. One of the scanned worlds had not gone to grey.

"Aurie, report. Is it the Hegemony?"

"Negative. Nanogenic survey systems have experienced an Invalid Topography Error while attempting to scan coordinates seven gamma by eleven epsilon by four rho."

Mira raised an eyebrow. She suddenly wished very much that Zekk had come with her. She knew her way around a computer, sure, but she would need the Reconstructionists' engineer for anything more than a typical malfunction.

"What is an Invalid Topography Error?"

"The system documentation reads that an Invalid Topography Error is thrown if the ANES is unable to establish the quantum boundaries of the target world. Administrator Zekk has left additional comments in the source code for this type of error. Would you like me to read them?"

A second blinking blue dot turned orange.

"Sure."

"All parallel worlds possess the same geometry in metaxic space. This error occurs if the nanites experience Boundary Violation Errors while attempting to access the target world. These would indicate the presence of a world with atypical quantum geometry. Such a world would still be theoretically accessible, but passing through the quantum threshold would be extremely dangerous. We do not know how well quantum ships would hold up when permeating abnormal metaxic boundaries. Damage would be possible."

Mira grabbed at the lever in the side of her chair and pulled herself upright. The holographic projection faded.

She looked out the viewport in front of her seat and scanned the metaxia with her eyes. Before her lay the usual coruscating hues of blue, twisting and turning into one another, interrupted every so often by little cracks of electricity, each tearing open a brief glimpse into the landscape of a parallel Earth. Nothing at all appeared unusual.

"Is the Liberalis currently pointing in the direction of the two worlds where we've experienced errors?"

"No. There are now three worlds that have generated Invalid Topography Errors."

Mira bit her lip. "Point us toward them."

She felt the ship's engines activate beneath the deck plates, and her viewport panned upward and left, coming slowly to a halt seconds later. She scanned the metaxia carefully with her eyes, but nothing appeared to be amiss.

"How far away are the worlds that produced the errors?"

"10.6 kilodivs."

A little over an hour's journey.

"Plot a course. I want to bring the Liberalis to a point in the metaxia 50 divs from one of the worlds that produced an error. But make sure that we keep at least 50 divs away from any of the worlds that have produced an error, or which haven't been scanned yet."

The holographic field reappeared, this time in front of the viewport, which Aurie helpfully dimmed. A line shot out through it, reaching out towards one of the orange dots.

"How is this?" Aurie asked.

"Good. Thank you, Aurie." Mira activated the helm interface and set her hands within it. "Engage."

Before she had left Earth, Mira and Arn had taken a trip away from Granite Lake, through the Snake River Valley, past the Tri-Cities, and down the old, derelict roads into the Yakima River Valley. They started in the late evening and arrived at the Tri-Cities at night, moving very carefully around and away from the periphery fence. Before long, the lights of the city had disappeared behind them, and the skeletal husks of ruined vineyards and ranch houses gleamed under the moonlight on one side of the road while the Yakima River burbled on the other. Some thirty kilometers out from the Tri-Cities, they found a derelict ranch nestled into the edge of the steep hills. It seemed like a good enough hideaway, so they broke a window, entered, and made a small bonfire in the back yard behind the library. The library's walls were lined with bookshelves, all empty, of course. One of them had even collapsed. They left the bookshelves where they were and chopped up the dusty kitchen table instead for the fire.

After eating their makeshift barbecue, they put some rocks around the fire and did a bit of exploring. The second floor had three bedrooms, each with all the usual items missing. Bedsheets had been taken, leaving bare and moldy mattresses. The rooms were vacant of socks, underwear, t-shirts, and jeans, but an assortment of less practical clothing lay strewn beneath mounds of dust. Cabinet and closet doors stood ajar. Some furniture was toppled. Nothing electronic remained. That had long ago been looted. And nothing printed remained either—not a book, a magazine, nor even a notepad. All that had been scrubbed away by the ideological cleansing, a perfect literary holocaust here in the Hegemony, death by a thousand revisions in the bi-coastal Equum.

At the far end of the second floor, they found a hatch in the ceiling with a cord attached to it. Arn pulled the cord, and a staircase retracted, leading them up into an even dustier attic. Mice squeaked and scattered across the floorboards, and a labyrinth of cobwebs connected various toppled boxes and broken pieces of furniture. At the far end of the attic lay a door which opened onto a small balcony, where they found a pair of folding chairs, washed clean of dust by the occasional rain. With a bit of pulling, they managed to unfold the chairs and set them up so that they could gaze out over the Yakima Valley.

"What do you think it was all like, before the cataclysm?" Arn asked.

Mira shrugged. "I don't think it was paradise, and I don't think it was hell either."

"Then what was it?"

"Probably a paradox. At least one thing seems certain. A lot of people were able to do whatever they wanted."

"Not like now."

"No."

A long silence.

"Do you ever wonder," Arn said, as he leaned forward and clenched the canteen he was holding, "about what we'll do with our library?"

"Protect it, of course."

"But what use will it be, if no one can read it but us?"

"Perhaps that was the mistake before." Mira crossed her arms and cast Arn an apprehensive look. "Presuming that literature needs a use."

"Perhaps. It makes me sad that we'll never know if it's truly ours."

Mira leaned back. "It can never be perfect, but that was never the point. Not even when we had ours. You should have read enough Plato by now."

Arn smirked. "Right. The story of the people in the well, right? In that dialogue about the optimal society. What was it called?"

"*Public Policy.*"

"Right. Didn't Plato think that the world of ideals was real, though?"

"Perhaps. But even if he did, wasn't he also skeptical that a person could ever fully comprehend the ideals?"

Arn exhaled sharply and smiled. "Probably. I suppose you're right. Getting there was never the point. The point was to try."

A long silence permeated the balcony as they looked out over the valley, its dark river churning somewhere distant, the same as it had for hundreds of years before, back when this house had contained a family, living what they thought had been a normal life, their library filled with shelves and shelves of books. Mira wondered if they'd appreciated what they'd had, made the most of it.

"Do you think," Mira asked, "that if we could get rid of the Hegemony bureaucracy and military—let's say we could make them all disappear overnight—do you think that we could get all the rest to care about Plato and Aristotle, and Herodotus and Descartes, and Spinoza and Eco?"

Arn shook his head sadly.

"And then there's what the Equum would do if they got their hands on our collection."

Arn snorted. "I imagine that sometimes. Plato would have to burn because he's a fascist. Aristotle because his classification system enforces conformity. Herodotus because he lies. Descartes because he's religious. Spinoza because he's sexist. And Eco for valuing 'bourgeois' semiotics over everything else."

"I think about that too, and I'm glad we're dealing with the Hegemony instead. At least the Hegemony is too stupid to understand any of what we're doing."

"But they'd still destroy it if they found it."

Mira nodded sadly. "To me, what the Equum would do is worse. They'd turn it against itself. They would mock it and warp it into doing something it was never meant to do. They would make it placate a vapid and ethically bankrupt philosophy."

Another long bout of silence passed as they watched the river and the stars. Somewhere, down by their rover, a bush rustled. Mira snatched up her scanner and Arn clutched his holster. The scan revealed it to be a fox, and she sighed with relief and held out the scanner for Arn to see. He relaxed and sat back again.

"I think maybe they weren't able to handle it," Mira said. "I think that before they might have tried to make people handle it. They tried to make everyone gods and it didn't work. It all just fell apart, and now we're left with the pieces."

"And not even our pieces."

"I make them ours." She shot him a look. "Everything I upload into the Liberalis I consider a part of ours, at the very least participating in ours. Do you ever look at the revisions when I get a new batch?"

"Sometimes."

"Do you ever watch Marcus Aurelius?"

"Hmm. No. I haven't recently. Why?"

"The first time I read him, he sounded so confident. So... strident. He struck me as a tad too militaristic. But sometime, I don't know, maybe about a month ago, I read him again, and he'd become humble, even self-deprecatory. I pulled up all the revisions and read how he'd changed after all my scans. It was eerie, like talking to someone on a parallel world who's an alternate version of a person you know here. They don't know you, but you kind of know them, and you have to keep reminding yourself that they're not necessarily anything like the person you have all these memories about. I had this moment of wondering if I should trust any of it, whether any of this was even worth it."

She let that sit for a bit.

"What do you think now?" Arn asked.

"I decided both Aureliuses—no, all the Aureliuses—were

mine. The one who wrote the self-confident *Reflections*, the one who wrote the more humble *Meditations*, and all the others in between. We're in a position not just to understand the great works of Earth, but a cross-section of great works of all the possible Earths, too. We keep this stuff safe, Arn. For the few people who will appreciate it, who can understand why it's important and treat it with respect. And we hide it from all the rest because it's dangerous in their hands."

"I want to believe that there are more people who could understand it, more than just the nine of us in the entire world."

"There probably are. But there's the problem of finding them."

"No argument there."

Arn took a swig from his canteen, and they sat in silence for some time longer beneath the stars.

As the Liberalis's engines died down from a rumble to a low hum, Mira parked her ship, turned off the helm interface, pushed herself up out of her chair, and gazed into the metaxia. It still looked perfectly normal. She glanced over her shoulder at the map of the substratum, which now contained a cluster of six orange dots. The monitors indicated that she should be looking directly at them.

A beep sounded from her other side, and her gaze darted to a monitor blinking red. All her reflexes shot through with adrenaline and the urge to escape surged forth. She instinctively reached out for the emergency escape initiator, but her reason managed to catch her just in time—the indicator was the communications systems, not the proximity alert.

She ran a quick scan for other ships and was relieved to see that hers was the only ship present. The communications light continued flashing. Mira took a deep breath in, then out, and connected the signal.

"Hello?" she tried.

"This is Admiral Trenton Lake of the United Metaxic Intersections speaking. Your ship has entered quantum space we consider our territory. Please state your intentions."

Mira gulped. "My scanning equipment experienced errors attempting to analyze worlds in this region. I was merely investigating. I'll be on my way."

"Your ship is similar in design to the ships of the Hegemony—" Mira shot through with fear. The Hegemony had scanned this substratum. It wasn't safe. Not safe at all. "—Are you from the same timestream as them? … Hello? Are you there?" Muffled voices followed.

Mira's hand stretched out toward the emergency escape initiator.

The admiral's voice returned. "The Hegemony attacked us, but we were successful in defending ourselves. If you could provide us with intelligence that would help ensure our success against future incursions, or better yet, negotiate with them, we would be very appreciative."

Mira held her hand poised over the initiator. "How long has it been since they were here?"

A moment of silence, and then, "About two months."

"You said United Metaxic Intersections. What is that? Some kind of collective of parallel worlds?"

"Not exactly." There was a smirk in the admiral's voice. "It's easiest to explain if you dock and see for yourself."

"Dock where—?" As she asked, coordinates appeared upon her computer panel. She looked out of the viewport, still seeing nothing at all unusual in metaxic space. Although, come to think of it, there was one thing amiss. In the area of the metaxia before her, there were no ripples, those little bits of electricity ripping open brief views into parallel Earths. Here, in this region, there was only the swirling blue.

"Where are you talking to me from, if not a parallel world?" Mira asked.

"Have you heard of the concept of a metaxic contortion?" Admiral Lake replied.

"No."

"We can explain it when you've landed."

Mira pursed her lips. She should not do this. She had a new treasure trove of literature. She should get it back to the others, get it uploaded, safe and sound, and most certainly the Liberalis was in need of repairs that only Zekk could perform. Not to mention a good scrub down. Was she in any position to negotiate with mysterious people who lived inside metaxic contortions, if that's even what they really were?

On the other hand, this moment held great potential. An ally against the Hegemony that—at least potentially— wasn't as crazy as the Equum or as stupid and selfish as any of the other minor governments on Earth. Could she go back to Earth and return here later? Probably not a good idea if the Hegemony had already scanned this substratum.

The situation had also piqued her curiosity, and that annoyed her. If she left now, she'd have to wonder for the rest of her life what a metaxic contortion was, what the United Metaxic Intersections consisted of if not parallel Earths, and whether or not Admiral Lake could, in fact, have been trusted. She did not like the idea of all those questions bugging her for the rest of her life.

And so, as much as she hated the idea of giving in to her curiosity, she found herself drawing her hand away from escape initiator, entering Admiral Lake's coordinates into the computer, and initiating the Liberalis's engines.

When the Liberalis traversed the boundary between the

metaxia and a specific parallel world, a roiling peel would wash across the viewport into the environment of that world. As Mira took the Liberalis toward the coordinates transmitted by the admiral, she observed not so much a peeling away as an omnipresent, hazy fading-out of the swirling blue, while the details of her new environment coalesced out of a monochrome fog.

The first details she was able to see were the walls. They seemed distant, enclosing an enormous space lined with walkways and stairs. Large devices studded the room at even intervals, at first just blobs in various shades of gray. But soon those forms became more distinct and gained color, showing stripes of brown and blue and studded with green stars—ships, Mira realized, dozens of them. And now she could make out people amongst them, some of them suspended below the ships, apparently performing repairs, others moving about the space, others talking to one another.

And the walls, ceiling, and floor—there was something unnatural about them. They appeared vaguely metallic, but also somewhat hazy, as though she were looking at them through a static haze. Her eyes couldn't quite focus on them. They shimmered blue as well. And were they wobbling? It was hard to tell.

With a jolt, Mira realized that her computer was receiving new coordinates. They indicated a specific part of the room where she should land. She entered the coordinates and continued taking in the room's details as the Liberalis hovered to the far end of the room and descended onto a brown circle. A group of three soldiers stood at its periphery, watching her ship.

With a jolt and shudder, the ship landed solidly on the floor of—wherever this was—and the engines spun down to silence. Mira grabbed up her pistol, then decided against it and threw the thing into the storage locker at the back of the bridge. She snatched up her tablet computer instead, deciding that would be more useful, stuffed it into her backpack and slung that over her back. She opened the hatch in the floor, descended the ladder into the belly of the ship, a dark and cramped room with poor lighting. She fumbled until she found the airlock hatch. It opened with a clank and groan. Upon descending inside, she hit another button which shut the airlock above her. A final operation involving simultaneously holding down a button and pulling a lever opened the door in the floor and caused a folding ladder to descend from the Liberalis, where it clanked upon impacting the floor.

Mira sniffed the air. The ANES would have told her if the atmosphere had been toxic, but the smells of different parallel worlds always interested her. This one was bland, even somewhat stale. Not much to it. But then, was this even a world? How to explain the strange look of the floors, walls, and ceiling?

Mira took a deep breath and descended the ladder. At the bottom, she turned, and her eyes met the trio of soldiers. Two soldiers holding weapons flanked the man who walked toward Mira now. She straightened herself, trying her best to look dignified despite her disheveled appearance and dirty clothes.

"Admiral Lake?"

The admiral nodded. "I am. And you are?"

"Mira Rous. I'm from a world about 120 kilodivs from here."

"Welcome to Intersection Thirteen. What brings you to our metaxic cluster, Mrs. Rous?"

"I'm a—" She had started to say 'collector,' but caught herself. That usually worked on parallel worlds. Was that safe here, though? She had to say something. "Collector," she finished.

"What do you collect?"

Mira could not help the adrenaline burst that surged through her. The soldiers must have noticed it, because they seemed to Mira to be grasping their weapons harder, incited to potential action themselves.

"How do you feel about fiction, Admiral?" Mira tried.

"It is… interesting, I suppose. Why?"

Mira flooded with relief. "It is illegal in the Hegemony."

"I see. And I take it you are collecting works of fiction despite that restriction."

Mira nodded.

"Well, I think you will find the United Metaxic Intersections aligned to your cause. We support the free enterprise of individuals to pursue what knowledge and artistic endeavors they will. You must have been traveling for some time. Would you like to freshen up?"

Mira clutched the ladder of her ship. "But the Liberalis—"

"Will be fine," Admiral Lake said. "And if it's the Hegemony you're worried about, we have fended them off once before, and we are confident we can do so again. Won't you come have a look around Intersection Thirteen? I have a feeling you'll be very much interested in our libraries."

"Libraries?" Mira blinked a few times. "Plural?"

"Intersection Thirteen has twenty-two libraries. And the other forty-seven intersections have even more. Books from over three hundred parallel universes." The admiral smiled proudly.

Mira had to clutch the Liberalis's ladder harder as she took in the enormity of that statement. She regained her composure and looked the admiral over once more. No signs of any kind of deception of indirection. If he were lying or concealing some unfortunate fact about his society, he was hiding it extraordinarily well.

"Alright." Mira released the ladder.

"Follow me." Admiral Lake turned and motioned for Mira to follow, leading her toward a door in the wall. The soldiers took up positions behind Mira, and she began walking too, one foot after the other, hesitantly at first, across the hazy blue floor that seemed to squirm and wriggle beneath one's gaze.

Mira had been scanning and collecting books for the Reconstructionists for just over five years. Before that, she'd been trying with only modest success to scrape together a living as the baker for the Missoula marketplace. She had been able to keep herself safe enough, but when the soldiers wanted free grub, one gave it. Mira remembered all too well what had happened to her parents. The only individuals who the military and police seemed to protect rather than extort were the President and his ilk.

It was on a foray into the ruins that she discovered the unthinkable. In the rubble and husks of one of the ancient buildings, she'd found a box. She'd taken it home, picked the lock, and discovered three books within—*Frankenstein* by Mary Shelley, *The War of the Worlds* by H. G. Wells, and *Brave New World* by Aldous Huxley. She'd locked her house up completely, wrapped herself in blankets, and read by the light of nanite lumens for two days straight. She read each through twice, and when she'd finished, she became determined to join the group of people who had shown her how to break into the ruins and salvage these ancient treasures, a group whose name she did not yet know, but whose members understood the power of books—the power to free oneself to really *think*, and not in the utilitarian way that the Hegemony wanted of its civil servants (that was the only way to live comfortably these days), but rather in the way that allowed one to explore new possibilities, to imagine what a better world might be like.

After days of arduous waiting, Enro and Hanith, the couple who had taught her ruin running, returned to Missoula with their leader Tirin and his son Arn. They happily accepted her contribution of three original books and introduced her to the means of recovering even more of what had been lost. She'd heard of metaxic travel before. Her mother must have mentioned it in passing during her brief and inadequately supplied secondary education (although she had to at least give the Hegemony credit for giving her what she needed in order to learn to read; as much as the Hegemony hated literature, they did need their populace capable of being manipulated by advertisements).

The Reconstructionists proceeded to try to teach her quantum mechanics and computer programming, but to her dismay, she had found the intricacies of those subjects had not come quickly to her. It had been Arn to suggest that she try her hand at piloting a metaxic ship, and her reflexes had proved much better than her aptitude for numbers.

One day, about a year after Mira had joined the group, Arn had taken the Reconstructionists into the forests of the North while his father had stayed and tended to the Granite Lake hideout. They had traveled far, perhaps even as far as the old Washington-British Columbia border, whose various checkpoints and station ruins still dotted the landscape. They camped in a secluded area, and together they read the newest updates to Earth's literature, not the Equum's offerings, which contained numerous inconsistencies and reeked of ideological cleansing. Rather, they read the literature that they were constructing, the one incorporating the newest works that Mira and Haden had just brought back from their visits to parallel Earths.

They'd spent the first night reading, and on the second,

they huddled around the fire while owls hooted and crickets chirped. The summer air hadn't cooled even with the setting sun, and they almost hardly needed the fire.

"The twenty-first century is still such a mystery, isn't it?" Arn observed.

"There's a kind of trajectory," Haden added. "Things get gradually better and better all over the world. And then there are two world wars, which the good guys win and everyone seems to recover from, except…" Haden trailed off and gazed into the fire. Seeming unsure how to finish his sentence.

"Except that the writers, philosophers, and poets go silent," Mira said.

"Not quite," Zekk said. "There was Arendt. And Eco. Le Guin, too."

"Sure," Mira allowed. "But they're the exceptions. And what about all the other details that suddenly disappear? Who was the forty-third president of the United States, and why do we only have fragments of references to Bill Clinton? Who was chancellor of Germany after Angela Merkel? What exactly happened in 2020?"

"A mass failure of public education, maybe?" Arn suggested.

"I don't see how it could all just *stop*," Haden observed.

"Maybe Gaia theory is right," Enna chimed in, "and systems of a certain complexity are prone to sudden, catastrophic failure."

"The Hegemony has proven stable enough," Arn said. Small laughs erupted, but even those laughing had to admit he'd made a good point. The Hegemony had dominated the continent for at least two hundred years. "Their bureaucracy is plenty complex. Same with the Empire of China. And unlike the Hegemony, we're pretty sure *they're* not lying when they claim a political lineage of over five thousand years."

Silence for a time.

Mira broke it. "Maybe it simply wasn't as good a time as their writing indicates that it was."

"Or," Enna again. "Maybe it was their very openness and egalitarianism that brought them down."

"It would, in a sense, explain the Equum," Zekk said. "I can imagine them developing out of a much 'softer,' less punitive and coercive version of themselves in the distant past."

The debate went on into the evening, but the experience stuck with Mira. She had always assumed that she had needed more freedom. When she had been a girl, she had watched her parents toil away for naught. She had stood by helplessly as Hegemony soldiers had shot them for their simple refusal to empty out their entire shop's supply and give it to them for free. Sitting under those stars, talking with her friends about books, about history, about humanity, about the state of the world, she had realized that she had come to possess all the freedom that she would ever need, and that freedom could exist together quite well in a world also containing the Hegemony and the Equum.

From the moment Enna had made her suggestion, Mira had found that her thinking on the old world changed. It was no longer a conundrum that the mystery century had contained a society-shattering failure for all its social and technological development—rather, it was how it had taken so long to all come crashing down, and why, as Arn had asked them, had the ones who could truly see, hear, think, and understand, so suddenly and unanimously gone silent?

-31

Dear Arn,

You will never believe what I've found. I can't believe what I've found.

Yesterday, after I finished writing to you, Zekk's program registered an error while scanning the worlds of this substratum. I went to investigate and discovered something called a metaxic contortion. It's a kind of artificially-generated pocket universe, inhabited by 630 million people who call themselves the United Metaxic Intersections. Apparently, each quantum twist is called an 'intersection' and each is its own pseudo-autonomous state. There are forty-eight of these things total. I've landed in Intersection Thirteen. They say they're the largest and most powerful, with over 80 million people just to themselves.

I've been here about twelve hours now. So far they seem pretty ideologically neutral, and they're fairly technologically advanced, too. They've been living in artificial universes like this for centuries already. They were founded by a group of humans who escaped from an Earth littered with petty and authoritarian leaders. They went into the metaxia and decided not to settle a parallel world, but to create their own parallel world. I asked why that was preferable and I got the kind of answer that I'd need you or Enna to make sense of. Something about the unlimited energy potential of quantum folds. At any rate, they seem to be able to generate as much physical space and power as they want. Their ancestors thought that was preferable to having to build up a civil infrastructure from scratch on a parallel Earth.

That ability to generate cheap energy and living space has allowed them to attract an enormous number of people from other parallel Earths. They seem eager for immigrants, and the government liaison they've assigned to me, a woman named Cathy, has already intimated multiple times about all their paths to citizenship. She said they even send out envoys and pick up people who want to escape tyranny on parallel worlds. And that is perhaps the most compelling discovery of all of this. Those immigrants have brought their culture and written works with them. Intersection Thirteen has literature from over three hundred parallel Earths.

But they've also met the Hegemony. That is my biggest point of concern. They've got a fleet of metaxic ships capable of fighting them off. All that Cathy has told me so far is that the Hegemony showed up and got into some kind of scuffle with UMI ships. It's unclear whether or not they have some ulterior motive with my presence, but the possibility seems extraordinary—a militarily powerful ally with a fleet of metaxic ships and hundreds of worlds' worth of literature? I know where your mind is going, and I've already told myself this a hundred times: It's too good to be true. It may just be, but I have to at least try to find out more.

Today Cathy is going to take me on a tour of some of their public spaces, and I'm going to have a look around their libraries. Then I'm going to talk to a politician of some kind, a 'senator,' I think Cathy called him, and I'm pretty sure he's going to want to negotiate for access to our defensive and engine systems. It seems they're about matched for Hegemony engines, but learning Zekk's tricks would give them an advantage. I'm betting they'll offer citizenship and a good chunk of their currency in exchange. I'll stall today so I can wait for your reply.

And don't worry, I've activated all of Zekk's defensive programs in the Liberalis. If they so much as nudge a molecule of the ship out of place, I'll know about it.

I'll write again soon.

All my love,
Mira

Mira looked herself over in the mirror. She was thankful that they'd given her a fresh pair of clothes, but brown was definitely not her color, and the design of the clothing was not to her liking either. Not practical enough, a bit too stodgy perhaps. She reminded herself that she was applying her standards to an unfamiliar culture and to be thankful for the gift.

Looking away from the mirror, though, reminded her once again of her novel environment. The walls of her small apartment, like all walls, floors, and ceilings here, shimmered blue and seemed to wobble if you looked at them too long. But they could be touched safely, were completely solid, and held one's weight as well as any other building she had been in.

Mira picked up her computer and headed out the door, which she locked behind her with a wave of her hand. They'd keyed it yesterday to her palm. She then headed toward the central corridor, where a few residents of the complex were also walking down the spiral stairwell, presumably off to their jobs. They wore clothing similar to hers, so at least they'd given her whatever was standard here.

In the lobby, she spotted Cathy Om, the government liaison she had met yesterday and had eaten dinner with. She was swiping through something on her computer but looked up and smiled as Mira approached.

"How did you sleep?" Cathy asked.

"Best night in about a week," Mira said. "Thank you."

"Would you like to get some breakfast?"

"Sure. That sounds good."

Cathy led them out the door into a very large corridor that extended into the distance on their right and left so far that the wall at each end was a distant blur. The floor here had a path lain down its center in bright red, which made it difficult to look at, as it contrasted sharply with the hazy blue. Perhaps that was the point. A tram hovered past, floating atop the red lines.

"Did they warn you about crossing?" Cathy asked.

"They did."

The ceiling here was high, too, perhaps about half a

kilometer above her head. All of the intersections were like this, apparently. Spaces had been carved out of the metaxia and connected to one another, not so much buildings as connected rooms. Here in the long room, Main Street, one could tell from the indentations in the walls just how tall the interiors of the adjacent spaces were. Lines and impressions waved about the hazy walls, some indicating interiors only a floor or two high, while others must have been skyscraper-tall, their indentations reaching up toward the ceiling.

"Is there a sky anywhere in the intersections?" Mira asked as Cathy led them down the busy thoroughfare.

"No. Some of our public chambers have been designed to simulate one, though. The Alesky Gardens, in particular, create the illusion of hydrogen-oxygen atmospheric firmament."

"How much interior space is there in Intersection Thirteen?"

"At present..." Cathy tapped at her computer. "542,393,977 square kilometers and counting."

"And counting?"

"We are constantly creating new spaces and renovating existing ones. Look there." Cathy pointed toward the outline in the wall across the tram tracks. Attached to it were metallic boxes, each spaced about a meter apart. As Mira watched, one box, every so often, would erupt in a fit of sparks. The boxes would also move every so often, jolting a few centimeters in one direction or another. "That one is the expansion of an existing space. We harvest potentia from the metaxic contortion at the core of the intersection and use it to carve out new spaces. Potentia is used to craft most of our tools and furniture, too. In a sense, even our food."

"Oh? Is the food made of it?"

"No. But potentia are responsible for the water and

electricity that allows us to run our agricultural and animal husbandry sectors."

"And it comes from the metaxic contortion?"

"Yes. Each intersection has a generator capable of harvesting energy from its contortion. My favorite metaphor for how it works is the rope. A rope is a bunch of fibers, right? Imagine you're holding them in front of yourself in both hands. All the fibers would be in a straight line. But then you start to twist them. The metaxia is the fibers, and the potentia are the energy generated when you the fibers rub against each other in the twisting."

"And the potentia can carve out new spaces? Wherever you need them?"

"That's right," Cathy said.

They reached a two-story outline in the wall, and Cathy stopped them in front of a door-sized portion of it. A sign clung to the wall above the portal, and Mira quickly translated it on her computer as they waited. The name of the establishment, it seemed, was *Golden Circle*. The portal shimmered, and the portion of the wall inside the outline vanished. A man walked out, followed by two women. Cathy waited for them to pass and then motioned for Mira to go inside.

Mira walked into a kind of cafe. The tables and chairs were normal enough, but there were no windows. Nevertheless, the room was brightly lit by nanite lumens affixed to the ceiling at intervals, and various pictures had been hung on the walls. In Mira's honest opinion, the artwork was hackneyed and tacky, but she appreciated the attempt to reduce the monotony of shimmering blue.

A waiter guided Mira and Cathy to a seat at the far end of the room, where they sat and were handed menus.

"Order anything you like," Cathy said. "Don't worry about the price."

Mira got out her computer, scanned the menu, and

looked over the translation. She had gone over their alphabet the previous evening, even drilled it for a time, and she couldn't help but notice something about the original text of the menu. She hesitated, but then decided to ask.

"I couldn't help but notice... Your currency symbol looks an awful lot like your letter P. Are potentia also your currency?"

"That's right," Cathy smiled. "Good detective work."

Was that an amused smile or a wary one, Mira wondered. She scanned her translated menu and decided on something called a trabulunta sandwich. Whatever a trabulunta was, Mira hoped it was good.

"I was told yesterday that you have books from three hundred different worlds. Where do your animals and plants come from?"

"Most are from Isallna. That's the name for the planet on the plane where the Founders came from. We've had a few other imports over the centuries. Rennian grain proved particularly durable. Last century, we discovered that Thelothoid fowl got along better with other farm animals than Isallnan. So, there have been some imports, some interbreeding, but it's still mostly Isallnan cuisine."

"Is there any political relationship with them? The government on Isallna?"

Cathy's expression dropped. "A bit. Some governments there allow us to recruit immigrants, others don't. I would call our relationship with most governments there neutral."

Mira decided to let that topic go for now. "Tell me about what we'll be seeing today."

Cathy brightened. "There's the Alesky Gardens, which I mentioned earlier. I'll show you the Municipal Exchange, designed by one of the Founders in the first year after we declared ourselves a sovereign state. Then we'll go to the Gyrospire, which is our generator and energy hub. And finally, Founder Square, the center of UMI government. Since I know you're interested in books, I'll leave you with instructions for how to get to the Intersection Thirteen Central Library. I hear you're collecting books. Is that right?"

"Yes."

"Your own world must have quite a significant contribution."

Now is was Mira's turn to frown. "Not anymore, unfortunately."

Cathy nodded and was about to say something, probably apologetic, but the waiter showed up just then to take their order. When he'd finished, Cathy began describing the history behind the places they were going to visit that day. Mira couldn't help but reflect on Cathy's naivete. How lucky, Mira thought, to be able to assume a society must be abundant in books.

Mira walked through the Alesky Gardens spellbound. Holographic emitters in the ceiling projected a realistic simulacrum of a blue sky and low, fast-moving wisps of clouds. The air was moist and botanically pungent. All around her lay a rainbow of flora—flowers, trees, shrubs, vines, and more. Birds flitted between the branches, erupting in varied bursts of chirps and caws, while butterflies drifted about, perching here and there amongst the greenery.

A circuitous path led through the gardens, breaking time and again, winding beneath an outcropping to one side and ascending upward on the other. The splits in the paths always seemed to meet up with one another again eventually, forming a circular route through the gardens.

The gardens were neither crowded nor vacant. A couple walked past them at one point, and Mira also spotted three families, in each case, parents with their children, but it was easy to move about, and she only occasionally passed others.

Cathy talked the whole time, explaining how one of the Intersection's Founders had wanted to bring a diverse array of alternate Earth flora together in the most beautiful way possible. At the time, it was believed that spaces within the metaxic contortion would only ever serve utilitarian purposes, and that, beyond basic agriculture, non-human organisms would never thrive. Charles Alesky had proven otherwise with the five square kilometer space he had purchased and cultivated.

What shocked Mira the most was not the difference between her Earth's flora and the exotic species before her—having visited one hundred seventy-six parallel Earths and counting, she was used to that by now. No, what shocked her was the ease and carefree attitude everyone on Main Street and in the gardens displayed. The families walked about with their children in tow through a public space in the middle of the day and without any obvious firearms or even the haze of protective nanite programs about them. In the Hegemony, such behavior was unheard of, and while the Equum provided such safety, moving about in their territory was fraught with a social brand of mortal terror. In the Equum, one dared not make eye contact with a stranger or speak to anyone unless it was absolutely necessary. The citizens of the Intersection seemed unburdened by either form of fear—could they be truly free? Mira could conceive of the state, just not how it was brought about.

The only places on Earth where Mira had felt capable of being herself had been in the abandoned places—the old houses in the Yakima Valley, for example, or far to the north in the mountains, the kinds of places her companions and fellow Reconstructionists often went. Places where normal people could go to talk and share ideas. Mira wondered, between deep breaths of the deliciously pure air of the Alesky Gardens, where the Intersection's crazies were. Where were the mobs of the ignorant demanding a supreme leader to fix all their problems for them? Where was the entrenched elite, callously demanding society conform to its ideology and ruthlessly punishing deviants even as the rules shifted hourly? Mira knew where to find both such groups and their respective power centers on Earth. All of the Earths she'd discovered in the metaxia had possessed one or the other, though the levels of success at suppressing them varied somewhat. How had this society maintained its stability?

She dared not ask, but she continued to observe. Cathy kept talking about Charles Alesky.

After the gardens, they walked to the Municipal Exchange, an elaborate building that possessed an exterior. Cathy explained that most spaces in the Intersections were simply linked to the other spaces with doors, and so the Municipal Exchange was one of the few true buildings. Elements of the quantum non-space had been left surrounding the hollowed-out interior to provide a kind of exterior, an elaborate latticework of the pulsing, hazy blue. They did not stay long in the interior. It was very busy, with men and women in formal-seeming dress running about, screaming into their handhelds, and looking up at enormous monitors which lined the walls of space and whose displays were constantly changing their letters and numbers. Cathy explained that it was all part of a complex system of exchange that had grown up around the generation of potentia. Cathy seemed enamored of the whole affair and waved her hands about towards various hubs of human activity while people darted around them, but Mira found the whole experience unnerving. Every time someone shot past here, it activated the flight mechanism she'd developed on Earth—'An attacker! Run away!' her mind screamed and she would suppress the urge just in time for it to happen all over again. Cathy seemed to notice Mira's unease and cut their visit short.

Next, Cathy took her to the Gyrospire. This was the largest open space Mira had seen in the Intersection, a room she was told was more than sixty square kilometers, one long, 500-meter diameter vertical cylinder. A throbbing cluster of tubules hung suspended in the center of the room. The tubes made Mira think of very large veins and arteries, especially the way they shifted and squirmed. Different parts of it oscillated different colors. At any given moment, some parts would be orange, others yellow, others green, the patches always changing. While most of the enormous apparatus looked mechanical, the throbbing multi-color tubules looked organic. Some of them must have been the width of her finger, while others were enormous, ten or twenty meters in diameter. The whole cluster of them throbbed. Light bursts erupted from them in fits, and the room smelled of oil.

An expansive network of metallic walkways and stairs stretched up and down, wrapping around the throbbing tubes, which extended downwards and upwards as far as Mira could see. Men and women in gray and blue uniforms moved about, some carrying tools, others working at panels set into the room's exterior wall.

Cathy proceeded with an explanation of how the potentia were harvested here and then shunted to the vast storage reserves in the Intersection Central Bank, which then decided how and when to release them into the Intersection economy. All the Intersections, it seemed, had their own gyrospires, but there was only one central bank for all forty-eight Intersections. All their potentia flowed through Intersection Thirteen before being distributed back out again.

"We used to let each Intersection manage itself," Cathy explained. "But there were problems."

"Such as?"

"We had a civil war. It was a long time ago."

Mira bit her lip and nodded. She made a note to herself to learn more about that.

Cathy took her then to another restaurant for lunch, where Mira ordered a meat dish. The texture of the meat reminded her of steak, which she'd had only once on a rare trip to the Equum. Cathy talked amiably the whole time, but now about nothing much in particular. Mira realized that Cathy's job must have been to make Mira feel comfortable, relaxed, to ply her up really good so that she'd spill everything she knew about Zekk's engine and structural reinforcement techniques. Mira had always been terrible at this kind of banter. She preferred the kind of conversation she could have with Arn and the others, not this hollow babble.

After lunch, Cathy showed Mira the way to Founder Square, a large, cubic space just down the street from Mira's lodging. Its entrance was guarded by soldiers wearing uniforms similar to the one Admiral Lake had worn. The cubic room contained six more cubic structures, each affixed to one surface of the cubic room, and each with ornate quantum-carved exteriors. While the four clinging to the walls were off-center and at varying heights, the two attached to the ceiling and floor had been positioned in the exact center of the space. The primary entrance stood at the center of the cube on the floor, where more guards stood and foot traffic proceeded steadily in and out. The cubes were connected by walkways, which protruded from the cubes' sides, connecting the whole complex in a lattice of blue tunnels with glass windows. Each of the six cubic buildings possessed a unique architectural style. One of the wall-affixed structures, Mira thought, looked almost Gothic. Another was adorned with Greco-Roman-like pillars. A third held figures of people. A fourth reminded her of art deco, with hard angles, circles, and arches. The one on the ceiling looked spidery, its exterior webbed out, while the one on the floor with the entrance had a stately air about it, its exterior stylized, but relatively plain and practical.

"Come here in three hours," Cathy said. "And show this to the guards at the entrance." She nodded toward Mira's handheld computer.

Mira looked down at it to see that Cathy had transmitted her a digital document.

"You'll be meeting with Senators Murray and Harden."

Mira looked back up at Cathy, a bit frightened. "Should I go directly to the library, then?"

"You are perfectly free to move about the Intersection as you will." Cathy seemed to take note of Mira's concerned expression. "Restricted or hazardous areas are all clearly marked, if that's what you're concerned about."

Mira shook her head. "Are they all safe?"

"Ah," Cathy said. "Yes. We have crime, of course. But, so long as you keep to Main Street, where your lodging is, and the other spaces immediately adjacent to Founder Square, you will be perfectly safe. Believe me, you'd have to walk for almost three hours to get anywhere even remotely dangerous. The Intersection Thirteen Central Library is out that way." Cathy pointed to a portal on the far side of Founder Square. "That goes to Darnem Street. The library is down that road, about a kilometer or so. But feel free to explore."

Mira perked up at that. "Thank you."

"It's been a pleasure," Cathy replied. "If you need anything urgently, you can call me from your handheld. I'm in your contacts in the application called Tele."

And with that, Cathy walked into the cubic building at

the center of Founder Square, leaving Mira to make her way to the Intersection Thirteen Central Library.

Mira headed out of Founder Square in the direction Cathy had indicated. The arched passageway took her out into a street much like Main Street, where she had started her morning. A tram buzzed as it hovered down the center of the corridor atop its red-lined path. The people moving about looked mostly like business people, though she spotted a few students and families as well. She still couldn't get over how calm everyone was.

There had to be a catch. All human societies had their problems. What were they here?

Mira was able to spot the library right away—another building. This one was shaped like a double helix, the strands composed of a the same blue exterior as the walls with windows affixed at regular intervals, rows of books visible within. Glass walkways shot through the middle of the double helix, also line with shelves.

Mira hurried inside. No one stopped her at the door, and no one seemed to be guarding anything, an utterly surreal experience for her. No library staff was visible anywhere. An escalator presented itself before her, a sign above it, whose words her computer translated as simply "stacks." A young man entered behind her, walked around her, and proceeded to the escalators. Mira stood, staring, her mouth agape for many moments before she remembered herself. One could simply walk in and touch, *hold* books? She'd been to worlds where one could have free access to bookstores, or where, within certain sub-cultures, permission to libraries was freely available, but free books to outsiders? To everyone? Equum libraries were open to everyone in principle, but in practice, only the most secure Equum citizens could traverse them without fear of reprisal, as the lists of "acceptable" and "unacceptable" books were in constant flux, and one definitely would not want to find oneself having shown an interest in something unacceptable.

The scene before her was unthinkable.

And yet, here it was.

She scanned the lobby for some method of cataloging. When she failed to find anything in her surroundings, she tried her computer, where she discovered an app capable of searching the library system. Before long, she'd found the index number for Plato and began to make her way there.

She proceeded up two more escalators and found herself amongst rows of books. Scanning for her index, she continued in a gentle upward spiral around the outside of the helix, down one of the central corridors, up a little bit more, and—

Mira stood, transfixed, her eyes watering. Her knees gave out and she covered her mouth, gazing at the miraculous shelves before her: Seven shelves of Plato. Seven more of Aristotle in the next aisle. Beyond them, a row of Xenophon, Diogenes, and someone she'd never heard of named Demosthenes. Hundreds of books from dozens and dozens of parallel Earths, more physical alternate versions of the same text than she had ever seen in one place besides the Reconstructionists' hidden library in Granite Lake.

She could feel the tears streaming down her face.

And… people moved about them freely… without a care. Did they know what they possessed? Did they understand what a great treasure it was? This hall of the library was silent and empty.

Her mind turned immediately to the great task before her. Somehow, she had to get digital copies. She had to get as much of it into the Liberalis computer systems as possible.

"*Public Policy...*" Mira decided out loud, wiping her eyes. She scanned until she found it. It had four alternate titles: *The Masterpiece Society, Society, Tripartite,* and *Republic.* That last one was interesting, Mira thought. She picked up a copy, and flipped through until she found the famous metaphor of the well... only it had become a cave. Interesting. Which one had been hers, she wondered, the well or the cave? She would have to get digital copies of all these texts to find out, but imagine the progress she could make! This one library of the UMI represented many lifetimes' worth of the exploration and retrieval she'd been doing.

Mira took a deep breath. Her negotiating goal was at least clear—digital copies of everything they had.

Mira took the long way down to ground level, walking all the around the edge of the helix to the very bottom. She thought the whole time about what she would do if the UMI allowed the Reconstructionists to establish a base of operations here. She reminded herself that she was jumping very far ahead. She hadn't learned nearly enough about this society yet, and, just as she'd told Arn this morning, situations that seemed too good to be true probably were. Her parents came readily to mind. How brief those happy years with them seemed now. At least, she thought, they'd be proud of what she had achieved. But after they were gone, very few had approached her with good intentions, and it had made trusting others hard. It had taken her a very long time to trust Arn—a very long time—but he had managed to earn it. She hoped the UMI could do the same.

She found herself walking down Darnem Street, the whole time lost in thoughts of the possibility of a better future for herself, her colleagues, and their own library. A very large, arched opening in the wall presented itself and drew her attention. Its periphery was studded with carved rocks, forming an archway. Etched into the keystone at the top was the inscription "Darnem Bridge."

Mira stepped through and found herself on a raised walkway. Below her lay a river, holographically generated, of course. It filled a cubic space, probably a kilometer square all around. At the edges of the wall near the entrance on both sides were grasses and rocks, the 'river's edge' which gave away its simulated nature by disappearing into the blue haze of the wall. This room, too, had a blue sky with low clouds moving quickly across it. Something was generating wind too, erupting in irregular bursts and blowing at her hair.

Mira walked to the center of the bridge, looked out over the faux-river, and let her mind wander freely as the wind whistled past her. How to find out more about them? The library would be a start, for sure. She needed to make sure tonight that she negotiated for more time. Maybe she should give away that technically and mechanically she knew very little, that she would send for Arn and Zekk, and that would give her time to explore the library. Perhaps she might even ask them directly—?

"Excuse me, are you the metaxic explorer?"

Startled, Mira turned. A man stood beside her, hands behind his back, not too close. Alarm subsided, but she remained cautious. He was slightly taller than her, with sandy brown hair, bright, blue eyes, and professional but somewhat disheveled clothes. His eyes shown with unreserved interest, and if Mira guessed right, a heaping load of naivete. The kind of guy, who, if dropped into the Hegemony, would find himself robbed or dead (probably both) within hours.

Mira decided to engage. "Yes. And you are?"

"Martin Venner."

"Hello, Martin. I'm Mira."

"Nice to meet you. Do you shake hands?"

"Yes." Mira shook his hand. "How can I help you?"

"I heard you're from the same plane as the Hegemony."

Mira frowned. "Yes."

"Are you here to help us defend against them?"

"I will if I can. That's not entirely up to me, though. What is your occupation, Martin?"

He smirked, leaned into the railing of the bridge, and looked down at the water. "You got me." Mira almost took up her martial arts stance, but Martin was grinning and brimming with excited curiosity. "I'm a reporter. A journalist."

"Interesting. What's your publication called?"

"*The Probability*."

"Is it politically oriented?"

"We like to think we hit the center more often than not."

"Do you?"

"More often than not. Tell you what. I'll level with you and cut right to the chase. The government makes a big deal about saving people from oppressive regimes. We're interested in those kinds of stories."

"Why's that?"

"Not everyone who comes here is necessarily getting into a better situation than they left."

"Oh?"

Martin shook his head. "These areas around Founder Square are nice, but if you saw how people lived in the Periphery... It's not pretty. Most of our immigrants end up there. And yes, most of the elite today can trace their ancestors back to immigrants who endured the same conditions or worse, but it doesn't make it all right that we force people to live that way in the present."

"Why can't they live here?"

"Not enough potentia. They literally can't carve out the space. One cubic meter here costs a couple thousand potentia. Compare that to around five hundred or so in the

Periphery. Go to a less prosperous intersection and you could find prices as low as twenty per."

"And what prevents them from earning more?"

"Staggering differences in income between jobs. The highest-paid executive makes thousands of times more than the lowest earners."

"We have a saying on my plane, 'the rich just get richer.' Does that sound right?"

"Something like that. Is that what it's like where you're from, then?"

Mira considered her words for a moment. "It's worse."

"Oh?"

Mira wondered how much she should trust Martin. She should certainly not tell him more about the specifics of the Hegemony or the Equum before she'd talked to the senators. "If I came here, from what I can see, I would probably be escaping tyranny into something better."

"What makes you say that?"

"Your library for one." Mira turned and looked up and down the bridge. "And him." She nodded towards a businessman headed their way from the Darnem Street entrance. "And them." On the other side of the bridge, a family was receding toward the alternate exit.

Martin furrowed his brow. "What about them?"

"They are walking around in public and they don't seem worried. And they're unarmed with no visible nanite defenses."

Martin paused. The bemused, adolescent exuberance finally seemed to fade from his eyes, as though he were finally understanding a bit of what Mira's experiences must have been like. "I'd like to learn more about your plane."

"Maybe later." Mira took a step back from the railing.

Martin jumped almost in alarm. "Maybe we could chat over coffee tomorrow. You will still be here tomorrow, right?"

"Depends on what I see in *The Probability* tomorrow."

"You won't see anything."

Mira pursed her lips. "Alright. There's a cafe called *The Golden Circle*. Do you know it?"

Martin nodded.

"See you there tomorrow at nine."

"See you then."

Mira turned to leave, but Martin called from behind her. "Hey, one more thing."

She stopped and half-turned looking over her shoulder, still poised to take off. "Yes?"

"What do you call the planet on your plane?"

Seemed harmless enough. She'd already told Cathy and the admiral, anyway. "Earth."

"Thank you, Mira! A pleasure meeting you."

Mira turned and left the way she'd come, turning over all the new information about the United Metaxic Intersections that Martin had provided.

After finishing with the senators, Mira made a beeline out of Founder Square, down Main Street, striding quickly, avoiding eye contact with everyone, though by now many people were getting off work, and they had heard of the new visitor from the same world as the Hegemony, and so there were indeed many eyes on her.

Two kilometers later, at its very end, lay the entrance to the hangar bay. The guards nodded their assent as she entered, and Mira hurried across the bay floor toward the Liberalis. With a tap at her computer, the airlock opened and the ladder unfolded, clanking against the hazy blue floor, just like last time.

Mira hurried up it, closed the airlock, opened the interior door, and clambered up into the cockpit.

She cast her gaze around the small space. Nothing had

been moved. Everything was just as she'd left it.

"Aurie?"

"Hello, Mira," the computer's voice intoned.

"Has anyone accessed you in any way since we arrived in Intersection Thirteen?"

"No."

Then either Aurie had been hacked covertly, or the UMI *had* had someone on Earth. But one thing remained certain. They wanted to maintain their military advantage over the Hegemony, and they now knew that Zekk was the way to do that.

Mira threw herself down into her cockpit chair and rubbed her hands over her face.

"Mira?" Aurie asked.

"Yes?"

"Would you like me to open the encrypted message composition terminal for you?"

"In just a minute."

"I've started a sixty-second countdown."

Mira kept bugging Zekk that sometimes Aurie was annoyingly literal. Zekk would just roll his eyes and retort, "He *is* a computer program." Although at the moment, the thought of Zekk being smart with her was something of a comfort.

Far too soon, the holographic text editor had appeared before her. She took a deep breath and started thinking about just what she was going to say to Arn.

-30

Dear Arn,

I feel so stupid. By the time you read this, they will probably already be on Earth. In fact, they might even get to you before you read this. If you are reading this, don't try to hide, just encrypt and safe-store everything as per the protocol. They will certainly find you, but they don't need to find the library. Even if they did, I don't think they'd care about it.

Here's what's happened today. They showed me around their city. Neat stuff. Impressive library. A phenomenal collection from so many different Earths. If we can ever manage to process it all, we'll gain decades, perhaps even a century's worth of additional accuracy to the library.

Anyhow, in the afternoon, I met these two senators, Murray and Harden. They didn't say how they knew, but they said they knew about Earth, its metaxic coordinates, about the Hegemony and the Equum, and about the fact that Zekk is the one who designed and programmed the Liberalis. I didn't tell them any of this, so it means they either hacked the Liberalis, or they've been on Earth already, and they just didn't expect to find anyone besides the Hegemony and the Equum. I'm mostly certain they haven't hacked the Liberalis. Aurie hasn't detected an intrusion, but that doesn't mean it didn't happen.

I feel like an idiot. Here I was, almost ready to trust them just a little, and it turns out that they're just as sleazy as I should have expected them to be. Although I met one person... a journalist named Martin. He might be alright. It seems like I'm stuck here for a bit, so I might as well follow up with him. Carefully. I'll take a look at his publication, too. He called it The Probability.

When they show up, just go with them. They've treated me fine so far. Their whole population knows I'm here, too, so if their media has any autonomy, they might be compelled to keep treating us well. And they still have all these books. Let's get what we want from these people and get away from them.

I'll do what I can to make the Liberalis computer tamper-proof, but I really wish Zekk were here. I suppose I'll get my wish fairly soon.

Love,
Mira

"Mira," Aurie intoned. "Mira. It is now fifteen seconds past the time you told me to wake you up."

Mira's eyes flitted open. She yawned and stretched.

"Mira, it is now thirty—"

"Yes, thank you, Aurie. I'm awake."

"I have other news."

Mira rubbed the sleep out of her eyes. Only five hours. She wished she could have gotten more. "What is it?"

"I have acquired a copy of the most recent issue of *The Probability*. I have also collated a number of other references to *The Probability* from other newspapers, particularly from editorial columns. It is supposedly a 'left-wing rag,' 'part of the deep state conspiracy,' and 'fake news.' Those are the most common correlations. Would you like to hear others?"

"Upload them to my computer," Mira said. While hardly glowing reviews, their impact on her opinion of Martin would depend on who was saying them and why. Growing up in the Hegemony had given Mira a healthy skepticism for impassioned political critique. People willing to crucify their political enemies didn't usually have the public's best interests at heart, not by a long shot.

She opened up the newest issue of *The Probability* on her handheld and began swiping through it. Nothing particularly toxic or extreme jumped out, to her sensibilities at least.

"Any articles by anyone named Martin Venner?"

"No," Aurie replied.

No luck there. Well, if she were stuck here for a while, she might as well make the most of her time, and besides Martin, there was still one avenue she hadn't explored yet.

"Aurie, I want to start a long-running scan. Search all available academic abstracts. I want to compile a list of people who are doing classical scholarship here." She and the other Reconstructionists read the works of fiction about twentieth-century scholars with particular reverence. The idea that academics could pursue knowledge and wisdom without having to fear for their physical safety and livelihoods seemed unreal. The numerous examples left behind by reclaimed authors such as Umberto Eco and David Lodge had indicated that the middle of the twentieth century had been a kind of halcyon of scholarship, even if those authors had been adept at showing how academic bureaucracies came with all the baggage of other human bureaucracies.

"Search complete," Aurie said. "No matches found."

Mira blinked. "How was it completed so quickly?"

"Scholarly abstracts here are indexed. I can search their key topics very quickly. In the last month, no scholarly research has been done on any classical era writers."

Mira frowned. "Expand to the last year."

"Processing." And then a few seconds later, "no matches found."

Mira tapped her foot against the deck. It was possible Aurie simply did not have the right access. She wondered if she would have better luck accessing the network from the apartment they'd given her on Main Street. She stood and stashed the handheld in her pocket.

"Start a search of the last century and upload the results to my computer when it's ready." She moved toward the airlock hatch, then added, "and if a UMI nanite so much as grazes the Liberalis's hull, I want you to contact me immediately."

"Confirmed," Aurie replied.

Mira scrambled down into the airlock, through it, and then down into the hangar bay. It was now empty and the lights had been dimmed. Not that any lights were particularly visible in the ceiling. Mira guessed that some kind of nanite mesh was generating each room's illumination. It would be a better simulation of a planetary environment than any other form of lighting. Beside the door to Main Street stood two soldiers, the only people present.

Mira strode toward them, watching them carefully. She passed through the door without so much as a flinch from them. Once she was far enough away, she let herself release her breath.

'They still want your technology,' she reminded herself inwardly. 'And they've probably figured out that they can't get at my ship directly. Not with Zekk's security systems.' The question was, what would they do to Zekk and Arn once they got them here? Mira had to remind herself to focus on what she could do next and not waste time blaming herself. Yes, she should have been more cautious. But the time for that had passed, and it was time to move forward. She had to keep her friends as safe as she could.

She entered the building containing her apartment and walked through the lobby. The attendant at the desk smiled and waved at her. She smiled and waved back. He went back to looking at his handheld. Mira strode up the central stairway, climbed the four flights, and arrived at the apartment they'd given her. She swiped her palm at the door panel, and its activation light blinked a bright cyan. It was still keyed to her, and she was grateful for this small bit of luck.

'Maybe they will treat Arn and Zekk all right,' she thought as the door slid open with a gentle hum. She strode in and sat herself down in front of the computer terminal built into the desk. She pulled up their internet and began searching for all her usual suspects: "Plato," "Aristotle," "Cicero," "Livy," "Marcus Aurelius," and the rest.

She frowned as the results poured in. A slew of independently written articles, most of which contained only surface details and mentioned the ancient authors as a way of prefacing some other topic. The range in quality of writing was mediocre to abysmal. Where did all the professional writers on the classics publish? She returned to the thought that perhaps those abstracts or indices weren't publicly accessible. She would have to ask Martin. If he could be trusted. Could he be trusted with that one? She weighed the pros and cons carefully. She'd already been much too open with these people.

Mira released a sigh. She glanced down at her handheld. Still only 7:30. Another hour and a half before she would meet him. She threw herself down on the bed and began taking notes on her handheld about how she wanted the meeting with Martin to go. Twenty minutes later she'd explored that topic to completion and turned her attention back to the issue of *The Probability* that Aurie had downloaded for her. She didn't understand a lot of the references, but the tone and character of the text was level-headed and factual. It didn't seem at all like what she considered to be 'fake news,' of which the Hegemony was constantly inventing new and extreme forms. The subtext of a number of *The Probability*'s articles was that the people who worked in government and business near Founder Square possessed far too great a share of all the generated potentia in the Intersections, and that Intersection Thirteen hoarded too much of other intersections' potentia for itself. Mira wondered just how politically dangerous this kind of journalism was. She couldn't imagine any periodical in the Hegemony lasting very long after posting anything remotely critical of the president or his cabinet members. The media back home was a vehicle for advertising products, nothing more.

Noting the time, Mira stowed her handheld, got up off the bed, and had just reached the door, when something caught her eye. She looked back around the room and realized that it had been the door frame by the bathroom. It was a bit hard to see, because the frame, being part of the wall, was composed of that blue, hazy blur that was difficult to focus one's eyes on. But as she drew closer to the door frame, what had been barely visible from the other side of the room became obvious—a part of the door frame had bulged outwards. Had the door frame always been that way, she wondered? No. She would have noticed something like that, even though the walls were hard to look at. The bulge was at least as big as her closed fist, perhaps a bit bigger. But it wasn't growing or moving in any discernible way. There was simply a bulge in the door frame where there had been none before.

Mira only momentarily reached out a finger toward it, but then she retracted her hand. Probably best not to touch it. Perhaps it *had* been there all along and she just hadn't noticed it, she wondered again. No. Absolutely not. She would have noticed something like that.

She backed away from the bulge toward the entrance to the apartment and turned away only when she had reached the door. She locked the apartment with a swipe of her hand and turned her thoughts back to preparing herself for her meeting with Martin.

When Mira arrived on Main Street, it was clear that the character of the day was markedly different than the day prior. This was more or less the same time she had met Cathy yesterday, and yet, far fewer people were out and about. The ones who were moved furtively, quickly, and single-mindedly. No one was taking their time, even a bit. Definitely not something like a weekend or more people would have been out enjoying themselves.

No. Something was up, but what?

When Mira arrived at the *Golden Circle*, she found that even the cafe staff seemed to be on edge, but they seated her regardless. She decided to use her time waiting to peruse the most recent copy of *The Probability* on her computer to see if she could glean any clues there. The front page had a title that seemed like a good candidate: "Largest Quantum Eddy in History Hits the United Metaxic Intersections."

She was familiar with quantum eddies. You couldn't just fly a metaxic ship in a straight line to where you wanted to go. If you did that, you wouldn't end up on the universe you were trying to get to. The metaxia, unlike normal space, seemed to shift every which way, as though the Cartesian coordinates making up its space were in a constant state of flux. It was part of what made her better at navigating the metaxia than others—she possessed an intuition for how to move her ship with the eddies instead of fighting them, making them work for her rather than against her. She couldn't explain how she did it. It was mere instinct.

But Mira understood the quantum eddies to be small, subtle shifts in metaxic space. What was a large one? What had happened, exactly? Mira read on. It seemed as though the eddy had damaged the potentia-generating systems of the Intersections, like the Gyrospire in Intersection Thirteen. But those effects normally meant only fractions of a percent of potentia lost. Occasionally, perhaps once every other decade or so, a larger eddy would wipe out a few percent of stored potentia. The largest one before today had claimed five percent of stored potentia and caused minor damage to the intersections' potentia systems. Last night's event had wiped out twenty-two percent of all stored potentia, and the Gyrospire was currently undergoing major repairs.

And then there was something else that caught her eye. The article called it "instances of metaxic intrusion." Reports were coming in from all over the intersections about bulges in the walls, like the one Mira had seen in her apartment. These, it seemed, were places where UMI space had been, in a sense, "reclaimed" by the metaxia. Potentia generation did not just go into people's accounts. It seemed a certain amount of stored potentia was required just to maintain the physical boundaries of the intersections' interior. With the stores suddenly reduced to seventy-eight percent of what they had been, the article claimed, the bulges had emerged as a kind of "metaxic rebalancing." Scientists believed that once the Gyrospire and other potentia-generating systems were back online, the phenomenon would go away and the bulges could be repaired.

"Good morning."

Mira jumped and realized that she'd been so absorbed in the article that she hadn't seen Martin approach. "Good morning." She tried to hide the article she'd been reading, but he'd almost certainly seen it.

Martin sat down. "Have you ordered?"

"Not yet."

Martin waved for the waiter, who took their order and hurried off to the kitchen.

"I see you're reading the top news of the day," Martin said. "What do you think?"

"I'm not used to thinking about quantum eddies like that. I didn't realize they could be so disruptive."

"No one usually thinks about them. We've known that an event like this could happen for some time, but we didn't bother to prepare. Hopefully, there will be some action on the other side of this. But I don't think you wanted to talk about quantum physics. I'm sure you know by now that our government is going to your plane to get more of your people and bring them here."

Mira nodded. "Should I be concerned about them?"

"I would be."

Mira bit her lip. "Are they going to hurt them?"

"Oh, no, nothing like that. But they are going to make your friends work for them and share all their technological expertise. They might offer them potentia, but it would be a minuscule amount compared to what private sector employees earn here."

Mira deflated. "That's it?"

Martin blinked a few times. "Your friends will be exploited!"

"But they'll be alive... and fed... and uninjured, right? How long do you imagine they'll have to stay here?"

Martin shrugged. "Hard to say. A few days, perhaps? Maybe a week or two on the outside. It depends how quickly the government gets what they want."

"And when they do get what they want, what happens then?"

"Well, I suppose, the government will let them do whatever they want here, so long as they don't break the law."

"Would they be able to leave?"

"Probably. I suppose it would depend if they learned any state secrets in their work. That seems unlikely, but I suppose it's possible."

Mira felt something inside herself burst free of her practiced restraint. Yes, she supposed Martin could be an elaborate decoy designed to lure her into a false sense of security, but at this point, she found that her mind could no longer sustain the level of complexity required of the supposed conspiracy to deceive her. Unless this whole society was absolutely insane, Mira decided, the secret police weren't actually about to jump out and jail her. They'd had so many opportunities already, and Martin had only further driven home their naiveté about what constituted an oppressive regime. It was well past time for the charade to drop. Mira had been bracing herself this whole time, and the "charade" was still going strong. It was becoming ever more likely that there was, in fact, no charade. They were simply an egalitarian democracy that knew nothing of real oppression. Go figure.

"Earth is so different from this place..." Mira said.

Martin leaned forward. "Tell me."

"Let's say this situation were reversed. Let's say you and I were on Earth right now, and you were the visitor. First, let's suppose we're in the Hegemony. They're the biggest country on our continent. They span most of the continental interior. So, we wouldn't be sitting in a cafe having this discussion. That would be flat out impossible. We'd have to find somewhere safe, like an apartment or a cellar, or a very special cafe, if you understand what I mean. Somewhere without surveillance, and there's a lot of surveillance. Presuming we did find a place to talk, if the Hegemony wanted information out of your friends, and if they could come into Intersection Thirteen and take them away, they would extract that information from them through any means available, and the simplest is torture—remember that the people running the Hegemony are really quite stupid—and then, if your friend didn't die during the torture, they would be killed afterwards. And that would be regardless of whether or not they were actually a threat, or even if they'd willingly helped the Hegemony out. Survival in the Hegemony means knowing at all times what is likely to piss off the people in power, and if you want to do things that will piss them off, you find ways of doing it very, very discreetly. Otherwise you, and most likely, all the innocent people around you, will end up dead.

"Second, let's talk about the Equum. It's a country split in two, one part on the west coast of my continent, and the other part on the east coast. There's a reason that my group, the Reconstructionists, have set ourselves up in the Hegemony rather than the Equum. It's because the leaders of the Equum are clever, and I've chosen that word intentionally. Not intelligent, not wise—clever. Ostensibly, they have libraries. Ostensibly, they have free speech.

Ostensibly, they have fair elections. The reason those things are all ostensible and not real is that anyone who is perceived as saying or doing anything that violates the rights of 'oppressed persons' is atomically deconstructed on the spot. And the most frightening thing is that the definition of 'oppressed persons' changes almost hourly. New psychological phenomena are 'discovered' nearly as fast. Individuals at the top of this system are constantly altering their physiognomy in order to be whatever the newest and hippest identity happens to be. No one dares to be critical of any story, any play, any artwork, any piece of writing, anything at all, for fear that the thing's creator will interpret the criticism as a slight against their individuality and claim psychological damage. Individuals with lots of money and social status are relatively safe from accusation, so long as they don't say or do something really stupid. But anyone without such status must live in constant fear for their lives. I have visited the Equum exactly once, and the entire time I was there, I talked to as few people as possible, and then only to get train tickets and buy food. I prefer my oppression up front and in my face. The Hegemony might be stupid, but at least they are not deluding themselves. They are honest about being a murderous dictatorship.

"So you tell me that the Intersection Thirteen government is going to make my people work for them? And they might pay them? Sorry, I'm trying to get worked up about that one, and I can't."

Martin seemed almost dumbfounded. "How did all that happen?"

Mira shook her head. "We don't know. It's been like this for as long as anyone's been alive, and we don't trust either the Hegemony or the Equum to tell us about our history. The Hegemony says that prior to them it was just savage wilderness everywhere, with tribes of people killing each other left and right. But then they also say that the Earth is only ten thousand years old. Like I said, stupid. The Equum says that before them, social oppression was rampant and everyone was unhappy. No one dares tell them that everyone in the Equum is still oppressed and unhappy. Those of us who collect books can tell that we used to have a vibrant culture with literature, philosophy, and ideas. And then, sometime around the beginning of the twenty-first century, it just... stopped."

Martin raised an eyebrow. "Stopped?"

"No more literature. No more philosophy. Plenty of media, sure. You can find tons of fragments of entertainment media and advertisements—so many advertisements. It might explain why the Hegemony is so obsessed with advertising, even though they don't need it. But no *art*. It's as though all the people who knew how to really think just went silent. We talk about that a lot in the Reconstructionists. It's a big question open to speculation and with no clear answer." Mira smirked. "You might even say it's our defining contemporary philosophical conundrum."

Martin had started taking notes, but Mira didn't care.

"Tell me more about the Reconstructionists," Martin said.

"Sure," Mira replied. "There are nine of us. Our leader is named Arn. Your people are off retrieving him and Zekk, he's our... well, he hasn't got a title, but let's call him our chief engineer. He'd like that. Anyway, we're trying to reconstruct all the literature we've lost. The Hegemony has made owning any literature or philosophy illegal. Almost everything from before the twenty-second century has been burned and deleted. We've managed to recover some of our own books, but not many. Forty years ago, when Arn's father was still alive, he had an idea. It seemed many of our books had been lost forever, but if he visited parallel worlds and retrieved *their* versions of those works, then he could use a computer algorithm to find all the similarities between those texts and cross-reference them against how far away those worlds were from Earth."

Martin smiled and nodded. "You're reconstructing Earth's literature by sampling other worlds' versions of the same texts." His eyes lit up, and he put down his pen. "Then… what we have here… It must seem immensely valuable to you."

Every instinct in Mira told her not to nod or to give any indication of an affirmative. But, she reminded herself, she was not on Earth. She was somewhere much more open. And so, she replied with a simple, curt, "yes."

"It's ironic." Martin picked up his pen and tapped it against the table.

"What's that?"

"Most people here don't read that stuff anymore. I'd be surprised if anyone does, really."

Mira felt taken aback. "But… I visited the Central Library yesterday. You have rows and rows of shelves."

"How many other people did you see there?"

A wave of sadness washed over her. "Only a few. I thought, maybe it was just because it was a workday. Are you telling me it's like that all the time?"

"I'm afraid so. And the few you saw were probably just there for a periodical, or to use the network. Most people are too busy making enough potentia just to make ends meet. No time for anything else. At best, at the end of their day, when they're really tired, you can get them to pay attention to something with a lot of fighting or sex, a television show or movie. Something exciting. There might still be some schools that teach ancient authors, but that's rare now. They're too busy teaching the skills that will help students get a good potentia-generating job. Is that how it happened, do you think?"

"What do you mean?"

"You said that your culture on Earth went dark. The thinkers stopped writing. Was it because everyone got too busy? They spent all their time with the busywork of ensuring food stayed on the table and their homes weren't reclaimed— or, whatever people in naturally occurring universes do to stabilize their shelters."

Mira let out a small, sad laugh. "Thank you, Martin. That might be the most coherent theory about the Great Silence I've ever heard." She wondered what Enna would think of that one. Her survival instinct kicked in, and she decided to test the waters just one more time. "I suppose you have enough information for an article now."

"I do."

"Will it make your career?"

Martin shrugged. "Hard to say."

"You're an interesting society," Mira said. "I don't sense cruelty anywhere here."

"We have it, but it's subtle. And it's all around potentia. Trust me, if you and your friends stayed, and if you couldn't contribute to the potentia-generating systems somehow, life would be very difficult."

"But no one would murder us?"

"Probably not. Almost certainly no one in the government, anyway."

"Enjoy this." Mira waved her arms out.

The waiter arrived just then carrying their plates. "Well," he smiled, "I certainly hope you do."

Martin laughed. They thanked the waiter and dug into their meals.

After breakfast, Martin offered to show Mira his office, and she accepted the invitation. They left the cafe and began walking down Main Street.

"What will you do until your friends arrive?" Martin

asked.

"I would like to get access to digital versions of your classics."

"That shouldn't take too long. Anything else?"

"Any time remaining, I suppose I would simply sit and read all the versions you've got."

"You make me want to read the classics."

"Oh," Mira said. "You haven't?"

"Afraid not."

"You're missing out."

"Where should I start?"

"Plato. Then Homer. Then Aristotle. That will keep you busy for a good while."

They arrived at Martin's office, and he introduced her to the other staff of *The Probability*. Everyone was pleasant and friendly. People seemed a little busier than usual, but the edge she had felt on the street earlier this morning seemed to have diminished, and now most everyone seemed to be going about their normal day.

One reporter in particular stood out.

"Mira, this is Julia Kemp."

Julia was a tall woman. She wore nice clothes but had not gone overboard, Mira noticed. Julia's eyes radiated intelligence and discernment. She also evoked a kind of friendliness that seemed completely unfeigned. Her desk was also the cleanest and most organized Mira had seen in the entire office.

"Nice to meet you, Mira." Julia shook her hand. "You're visiting from… Earth, did I get that right?"

"Yes," Mira smiled. "Nice to meet you, too."

Julia turned to Martin. "Don't worry, Martin. The article is all yours. But perhaps, after you've published it, we could all get dinner sometime." She turned to Mira. "If you'd like, of course."

"That would be nice," Mira said.

Martin, she noticed, seemed somewhat bemused at the suggestion. Not upset or worried, but not exactly excited either.

When they had finished going around his office, she found herself back at his desk. "I suppose I should let you get to work on your article. Am I going to see it in tomorrow's issue?"

"Most likely."

"Am I going to like it?"

A pause. "I don't think you'll *dis*like it. You'll have to tell me what you think. Breakfast again tomorrow?"

Mira found herself smiling. "Sure. See you then."

As she walked out of the office and down onto Main Street, she huffed and chided herself. Was she letting this get out of hand? No, she decided. She was not letting this get out of hand. Martin was the best way to learn about UMI culture. She had to keep that advantage. No need to explain to him about Arn. Arn would be here soon enough, anyway.

She took off down the street toward the Central Library, turning her thoughts back to higher matters.

Once, back on Earth, Mira and Arn had decided to take one of their trips, this time to the giant volcano caldera in a place called Yellowstone. Some scientists believed it was ready to erupt at any time. Hegemony scientists weren't very good though, as they all tended to bend data in the direction that their leaders wanted it to go. So, either the volcano was about to blow any decade now, *or* it was in Hegemony leaders' interest for people to think that. There was no way to tell which.

Regardless, the mountains and forests were gorgeous, and the Hegemony did still maintain all the roads. Most parts of it were natural preserves, so they would be relatively devoid of both people and drones. The perfect place for them to really talk.

They found a lake in the mountains and set up camp. Arn would go swimming in the lake at sunrise, and then they would both go for a hike. Mira took pictures of the birds, and Arn collected up different kinds of leaves. He would image them later for a collection. It would be a book he would be allowed to print—neither fiction nor philosophy, such a book would be legal. A book about leaves. Completely harmless. Nothing to see here. Yes, Mister Drone, you may have a look. No need to incinerate it. No dangerously subversive ideas. Just a record of the beauty of our natural world.

They talked about where the Reconstructionists were going, what they wanted to accomplish, whether their estimates of the fidelity of their reconstructed texts were accurate or not. Arn could not question such things openly with the rest of the group, but Mira kept his confidence.

In a particularly tender moment one evening, in front of a fire on the gravelly edge of the lake, just as the last rays of light faded from the halo around the mountain peaks, Arn began talking about his father. Tirin had cast an oppressively long shadow, and Arn did not think he was dealing with it well.

"There was so much he did for me when he was alive," Arn said. "And I was such a jerk… about everything." Arn had been only nineteen years old when his father had been captured by Hegemony police in possession of a reconstructed copy of Mary Shelley's *The Last Man*. Nineteen was a terrible age to lose a father. Just old enough for him to have fully rebelled without yet realizing any of the myriad ways in which he was still quite an idiotic child.

"You have done *so much* for the Reconstructionists," Mira assured him. "You need to give yourself credit for that. He would be proud of everything you've accomplished."

"Mira," he said, with a twinge of fear in his voice. "If you ever... think twice about wanting to be with me, I want you to tell me. I will have trouble if I find out... a different way. I need there to be honesty between us. I know we don't expect honesty anywhere in the Hegemony, because it's an empire built on lies, but I can't have lies between the two of us. Can you do that for me?"

"Yes," Mira said. "I can. And if that ever happens, I promise I will tell you."

-29

Dear Arn,

It seems that you won't be coming here after all. I swear, I keep waiting for the other shoe to drop, but instead these people's behavior just keeps getting weirder.

The first thing I noticed yesterday was that everyone was walking around really tense, and there didn't seem to be as many people out and about. It turns out that all of these metaxic contortions that contain the intersections are susceptible to the quantum eddies that make steering in the metaxia a challenge. Last night, the Intersections were hit by a big one, the biggest one they've ever seen, and it caused a lot of damage.

As the day went on though, things started to calm down. I saw more people out when I was leaving the library and walking toward the Liberalis, but then later, when I got to my ship, I got a transmission from the senators I'd spoken to yesterday. They said that the ships sent to get you had been recalled to the Intersections and that your visit had been 'indefinitely delayed.' I thanked them for the information and asked if they had any further instructions for me. They told me I could continue to move about the Intersections as I wished.

Immediately after that, I scoured their media for more information. Big governments, even big egalitarian, democratic governments, do not just up and cancel major defense initiatives for no reason. I didn't find anything definitive, but it sounds like some of the scientists here are concerned about lasting damage from the eddy that hit this place last night. I didn't quite understand all the technical details, but I think I got the basic gist of it. The eddies disrupt the ability of a metaxic contortion to hold its shape. When a small eddy hits, they throw some energy at it, something called potentia (it doubles as their currency), and the problem goes away. This strategy has worked for almost three hundred years. But, it seems they've dumped a ton of potentia into trying to patch up the damage from this eddy, and they're still having issues. Exactly what, I couldn't say.

Anyhow, I'm just glad you and Zekk aren't imminently arriving here after all. It will give you both some time to figure out how you want to deal with the Intersection government if and when they eventually show up. They've treated me extraordinarily well, much better than I would have expected any government to treat me. But I find the people here naive in so many ways. Their political parties seem to get excited over the most trivial matters.

But, that's hardly my problem. What matters to me is that there's a treasure trove of ancient literature here from hundreds of different worlds. I went to their Central Library yesterday to get access to the digital versions of the literature, and it turned out they didn't have any. They've got a lot of their contemporary literature in digital form, but nothing more than about a century old. I asked why, and they said there was no demand. I asked if I could check out books, and it seems I don't qualify for a library account. I would need to become a citizen.

This is why I really wish you and Zekk were here. I need the scanner program modified so that it's capable of going through the interiors of about a thousand books lined up in rows of shelves. I'm out of my depth on that one. I'll keep doing what I can to get those books uploaded to the Liberalis.

They've given me no reason to believe I'm in any danger here. Let's hope it stays that way.

Love,
Mira

"I am sorry to wake you, Mira." Aurie again. "But you have an incoming transmission from Founder Square."

"Lights." Mira rubbed her eyes and pulled at the latch that caused her bed to incline upwards into a chair. The lights burst on, illuminating the still dingy cockpit of the Liberalis. "What time is it?"

"It is 3:22 am."

"The Intersection government is calling me at three in the morning?" Mira winced.

"That is correct."

Mira was getting thoroughly annoyed with these people. "Put them on audio only."

A voice erupted through the speakers in the Liberalis cockpit. "Ms. Rous?"

"Aurie, volume," Mira instructed.

"Sorry, come again?" the voice asked, the volume much better this time.

"Apologies, those were instructions to my computer."

"Good morning, Ms. Rous. Sorry to have woken you. This is Senator Murray. We met the other day."

"Yes, I remember. And that's all right. What can I do for you?"

"We urgently need to know if you or any of your compatriots has any particular skill in the fields of quantum physics or metaxic spatial mechanics."

Mira paused. She decided she would ask. "And this question couldn't have waited four hours?"

"No, ma'am. I'm afraid not."

Mira blinked a few times. "Senator, should I be concerned about my safety in the UMI?"

"Not at this moment, no. But if you have any contacts on any plane with advanced expertise in quantum physics or metaxic spatial mechanics, we can make it well worth your while if you were to introduce us to them."

"I'm afraid I can't think of anyone who fits that description. I've sought out mostly literary types in my expeditions. And as for the other Reconstructionists, they aren't going to teach you anything about the metaxia that you don't already know. No one on Earth has ever heard of a metaxic contortion, let alone tried to stabilize one."

"Thank you, Ms. Rous. I apologize for the interruption."

"No problem. Goodbye."

"Goodbye." The senator ended the call.

—

Mira did not go back to sleep. She spent the next two hours scouring Intersection Thirteen's media for further evidence of what the hell had gotten the Intersection government so worked up.

Apparently, the elevated concern was over the fact that, despite the Gyrospire and other potentia-generating systems coming back online stronger than ever, new metaxic intrusions were still being reported. One periodical had started running a series of graphs on its front page, one for each of the forty-eight intersections, which showed the number of new reported intrusions per hour. The most populous intersections—2, 7, 13, 18, 19, 24, and 35—had their graphs highlighted prominently, and in those intersections, there had been a definite uptick in instances of the intrusions. Intersection Thirteen had reported two new intrusions per hour immediately after the eddy, four new intrusions per hour by the end of the day, and the number was now down to three per hour, but the author of the article noted that this number was alarming because of the time of the evening. He expected many new intrusions to be reported when people woke up and began examining their living spaces.

Mira put down her computer. That would certainly be a government-scrambling kind of problem. You have a typical kind of event, but it's the biggest one of its kind you've ever seen. You think you know how to deal with it, but it has an effect that none of the others have had. The eddy itself had gone, they'd repaired the damage to their systems, but the metaxic intrusions weren't stopping. Why?

The senator's question indicated that they didn't know.

Funny, Mira thought, how her opinion of the UMI had changed so rapidly in the course of just a few days. It would now suffice just to get those books and get the hell out of here.

All at once, something struck her.

"Aurie, I want you to run a simulation for me."

A familiar click and hum erupted from the computer core. "Ready for inputs," Aurie said.

"Take the data in the graphs from the front page of... *The Intersection Twenty-Four Post.* Assume that each intrusion eats up an area of space about the size of my fist. Let's say one cubic decimeter. Calculate the amount of time it would take the Intersections to lose all their interior space. Assume each intersection is as big as Thirteen is. Cathy said that was about half a billion square kilometers."

Aurie clicked and buzzed a bit. "There is yet insufficient data to determine whether or not the phenomenon is progressing at a linear or an exponential rate. Which model shall I infer?"

"Run both."

More clicking and buzzing.

"If the intrusions increase at a linear rate, then it will take approximately one and a half years for all space in the Intersections to be eliminated."

"And what if the rate is exponential?"

"About twenty-nine days."

Mira gulped. "What information is available about the metaxic transport capabilities of the Intersections?"

"There is some data available in public records."

"Scan them. Tell me how long it would take to evacuate all 630 million UMI citizens."

More clicking and buzzing. Minutes passed. Mira tapped her foot and bit her lip. She was beginning to understand why she'd been woken up.

"The following calculation possesses an estimated fifteen-percentage-point error in either direction. Apply this information with caution. It would take the United

Metaxic Intersections 183 days to evacuate all of its citizens to the nearest habitable Earth."

Mira could do 183 minus 15 percent well enough in her head. If the phenomenon was increasing exponentially, then the government of the UMI had no way of evacuating everyone in time.

New plan, Mira decided. She would get the books and get the hell out of the UMI. Even if she couldn't check out the books, she could try arranging groups of them in a vertical stack, which would allow her handheld computer to scan them. It would be tedious, but it would work.

There were also all the other intersections' libraries to think about. Mira got to work and crafted the template of an email to a library head, asking for digital access to all of their ancient literature. She then went on the web and found the names and emails of all the head librarians for intersections one through forty-eight (thirteen exclusive), and sent a copy of her request to each one.

When Mira looked up at the clock, it was 6:30. She felt exhausted, but adrenaline had thoroughly kicked in, so there was no going back to sleep now. All at once, she remembered her meeting with Martin; she had nearly forgotten about him and *The Probability*. She pulled up today's copy on her tablet and scanned for an article. There was one article penned by him, but it was about the metaxic intrusions rather than her visit. His story about Earth seemed to have been preempted. Not that it bothered her much.

A plan formed in her mind: meet him for breakfast at *Golden Circle*, then go to the library, which wouldn't open until 9, anyway. The UMI clothes she had been given needed a wash anyway. After two consecutive days of wear, they were starting to feel grungy. There had been a washing and drying machine in the apartment on Main

Street. She could stop off there first.

Mira grabbed up her computer. "Aurie, same protocol as yesterday. If any UMI nanites come near you, you transmit immediately."

"Protocol confirmed."

She scurried down through the airlock and out into the hangar bay. When she reached the floor, she kept her grip on the Liberalis's ladder and scanned the walls of the hangar. No intrusions here. Perhaps they would end up slowing down after all? She didn't actually know whether or not they would increase exponentially. This was a new phenomenon, and there was only about a day's worth of data. Perhaps the UMI researchers would find a way to stop it from spreading.

Mira hurried away from the Liberalis, clutching her computer tightly to her side.

The guards stood at the entrance from the hangar to Main Street. They glanced at her as she passed but did not bother her. As it was early, there were not many people out and about, but the ones who were moved about furtively again, a return to the state of things as they had been the prior morning. Over the course of the prior day, the citizens had seemed to loosen up, and more people seemed to be going about their daily business in public. This morning, the tension had returned full force.

One block away from her apartment building, Mira spotted a cluster of bulges protruding from the fifth floor of the outline of a space on the other side of the street. There were about five of them, one of them the size of her head and three more around it, fist-sized.

Mira hurried onward, into her apartment building—the staff once again nodded and smiled—up the stairs, and into her apartment.

With a swipe of her hands, the light came on, and her breath caught in her throat. The bulge in the doorway to the bathroom had ballooned so large that it now filled most of the doorway. It had become a sphere perhaps half a meter in diameter. Other smaller spheres dotted its surface and had appeared on the surrounding wall. On the opposite side of the room, another bulge had formed in the wall, this one fist-size, and two smaller ones had appeared beside it.

Mira crept toward the three new intrusions. There was something odd about the larger one. It appeared to have grown through the painting that hung on the wall. Mira reached out toward the painting and tugged at its frame. She watched the corner that touched the intrusion, and as the painting came away, she realized that a corner of the painting frame was gone. The intrusion had sliced it cleanly out of existence. The intrusion had not simply pushed the painting away from the wall as it had expanded, it had absorbed or obliterated the molecules of the painting.

Mira let go of the frame, letting it clatter against the wall, and backed into the center of the room. She took a few deep breaths and decided to focus on her goal—get clean clothes. But that would require moving into the bathroom around the enormous intrusion and then waiting there for an hour for the wash and dry cycles to finish. No. The intrusion could expand further and trap her in the bathroom. Best not to risk it.

She took off out of the apartment, headed down Main Street, came to *Golden Circle*, and asked for a seat. The staff seemed to recognize her, smiling as they seated her and brought her the same coffee she'd ordered the two days prior (they called it "lelkcha," but it was brownish-liquid made from the grinding of some kind of bean, so Mira had been calling it coffee, to herself, anyway).

She pulled up her computer and decided to go back to *The Intersection Twenty-Four Post*. The graphs on the front page had been updated. Now that people had been waking up, the numbers of intrusions reported had jumped. It was also becoming apparent that the intrusions were clustered. The presence of an intrusion in an area meant it was more likely that a new one would form nearby. Some areas were virtually absent of them, but in others, large clusters of them were forming, like the ones in Mira's apartment.

Mira pulled up her email and fired a message off to Cathy letting her know about the cluster in her apartment.

She returned to the article in the *Post*. It seemed the scientists had been conducting experiments, and there was a theory about how they could stop the phenomenon from spreading, but it would require testing. In the meantime, citizens were being advised to stay away from areas with the intrusions and to report any new occurrences to the authorities.

"Morning." It was Martin's voice.

"Good morning."

Martin sat down across from her. "How did you sleep?"

Mira shook her head. "Senator Murray woke me up at 3:30."

"Oh?"

"He wanted to know if I knew of any experts in quantum physics or metaxic spatial mechanics."

Martin nodded sadly. "Not surprising."

Mira's turn to look inquisitive.

Martin shrugged. "We've let the rich hoard all of the potentia, when we could have diverted it into research about the intrusions and many other things."

"You mean… you knew this could happen?"

"Mm hmm. The Founders knew of it as a theoretical possibility. But no one had ever seen it happen, until now."

"What does the theory say should happen next?"

"The intrusions are space that is metaxic again.

Contortion space that has been 'unwound,' to use the rope metaphor. You've heard that one, right?"

"Cathy mentioned it, yes."

"Well, those unwound areas exert an unwinding force on all the space around them."

"So they'll keep growing."

"Oh yes."

Mira spoke next in a whisper. "I'm surprised people aren't rushing for the hangar."

"It's not real yet."

Mira furrowed her brow. "What does that mean?"

"We've had our share of problems here. We've been at war with parallel worlds. Hell, we've been at war with ourselves. Twice. It's been a long and difficult three hundred years, but for the past century, everything's been stable, and the government, for all my complaints about how they manage things economically, has kept the food cheap and the power flowing. People are comfortable. This isn't a complete surprise. We always knew it could happen. The thinking now is that the scientists will figure something out, and things will go back to normal."

Mira looked at the table. "On Earth, we would never make such an assumption. But I guess people are too used to things just falling apart, rather than remaining stable."

"It's too bad I didn't get to publish my other story," Martin said. "The one based on our conversation. I can send it to you if you'd like."

Mira perked up. "Yes, thank you. I'd like to read it."

"What are you going to do now?"

"There's the matter of all your ancient literature. I'm going to go to the Central Library today and start scanning everything into my computer. Did you know that none of the classics have been digitized?"

"That doesn't surprise me."

Mira raised both eyebrows and stared at him

momentarily before blinking again.

Martin shrugged. "Like I said yesterday, demand for those books is low. Digitization priority is given to the books that circulate most widely. What will startle you most, I suspect, is the fact that all that stuff you see on the shelves, that's actually just a fraction of what we've got. There are a ton of really old books that the libraries don't keep in circulation because it's not popular enough."

"You mean... It's just sitting in boxes, somewhere. In storage?"

"Something like that, yes."

Mira put her hand momentarily over her mouth, then retracted it and took a deep breath. "But it's precious."

"It would be nice if more people here agreed with you on that, but they don't. Frankly, I don't know how the Central Library manages to give old books the shelf space they do."

"The Central Library said I had to be a citizen to check books out."

Martin looked around the cafe, then reached into his satchel and retrieved his computer. He tapped at it for a few moments, then put it away. Mira's handheld computer buzzed.

Martin leaned forward. "Those are my login credentials for the library system. Last I checked, the maximum number of books a person could check out was twenty. Choose carefully."

"Thank you, Martin."

A kind of buzzing screech erupted from the hallway leading to the kitchen. A flurry of sparks erupted, and a small cloud of black smoke appeared. Staff screamed, and everyone in the cafe looked toward the noise. As the smoke dissipated, a bulge in the ceiling appeared, it had intersected and half-absorbed a now inactive nanite lumen.

74

Mira and Martin returned to their conversation and eventually ordered breakfast. Mira tried to enjoy it the best she could. She had a strong feeling this would be her last breakfast at *Golden Circle*. Martin did not seem nearly as concerned.

After breakfast, Mira strode down the street as quickly as she could take herself without drawing any attention. She spotted two more intrusion clusters on her way to the Central Library, but she breathed a sigh of relief to see that the library itself had not yet been affected, at least not its exterior.

Mira hurried inside and made her way to the classics section. It was as deserted as it had been two days prior. She pulled out her computer and got to work, taking the books off the shelves, preserving their order, and stacking them on the floor, making certain that the lower-left corner of each was in alignment with all the others. Once she had a stack of twenty or so, she placed her computer atop the pile, pressed the scan button, and waited. A minute or so later, the familiar chime would ring, and she would retrieve her computer, return the books to the shelf in order, and start on the next set of twenty.

By midday, her stomach had started growling, and she considered getting lunch. She pulled up the *Intersection Twenty-Four Post* and checked the numbers of intrusions. The rate of new intrusions was still increasing. In Intersection Thirteen, they had reached fourteen new intrusions per hour. Mira decided to ignore her stomach and continue scanning. If Marcus Aurelius could find the energy to run a sprawling empire, command an army, and simultaneously write one of the greatest works of philosophy in history, certainly she could work through a little bit of hunger to get that many more books.

She worked harder, pulling books and lining up their

corners faster than she had before, willing her body to keep going. She had until five to scan as many books as she could, and she would do just that.

Finally, at exactly 4:43, Mira came to the end of the library's classics section. She had not seen one single other person all day, not even one of the library staff.

All at once, Mira remembered that she possessed Martin's library account credentials. She should have also asked him how to check out books. And then there was the fact that she hadn't brought anything to carry books in. She wasn't about to carry a stack of twenty books back to the Liberalis in her bare hands. She'd have to settle for three or four. She made quick selections—Aristotle's *Politics*, Ovid's *Fluctuations* (here called *Metamorphoses*) which would be a gift for Arn, and Marcus Aurelius's *Meditations*, a gift for Zekk.

She hurried down to the lobby and wandered for a bit until she found a row of kiosks with a helpful sign next to them explaining how to check out the books. After running the books through a scanner, she entered Martin's credentials, and the terminal displayed a green notification with a polite 'thank you' message.

Mira hurried out of the library and back to the Liberalis, spotting four or five new intrusion clusters along the way. She entered the hangar bay and was glad to see that it, at least, had still not been affected.

Upon entering the Liberalis's cockpit, she moved to the very back and waved her hand along the wall, then touched her left forefinger, her right thumb, and then her right ring finger into a scanner. An optical scanner shot a beam of bright light momentarily into her eyes, and with a great clank, a large metallic slab of the wall about two decimeters thick slid up to reveal a cubby. Mira stashed the books inside, and with a swipe of her hand, the safebox sealed itself.

She strode back to the cockpit.

"Aurie, ship status."

"Scanning... All ship systems are operating within established parameters."

"Tell me if you can do something, Aurie." Zekk had given Aurie some metaprogramming capabilities, but they were rudimentary. If you wanted to try to speak out a program, asking him if 'he could do something' was how you got started. "If the Liberalis loses any structural integrity at all, immediately initiate the engines, retract the landing gear, and get the ship into a hovering state. If I'm in the ship, then try to enter the metaxia. If I'm not, send an alert to my computer and repeat it every minute until I return to the bridge. This program should constantly monitor the ship's structural integrity and deactivate once the ship has entered the metaxia. Any prompts that normally require my input should be supplied defaults while it's running."

The computer core started humming beneath the deck plates, which usually happened when she tried this. Aurie wasn't typically successful at metaprogramming procedures. Zekk dumped most of his energy into metaxic engine efficiency. The fact that Aurie existed at all was a tribute to Zekk's dedication.

"I can do that," Aurie intoned.

"Excellent. Thank you, Aurie."

Mira went to the lockers at the back of the cockpit and retrieved two packs of field rations. She threw herself down into the cockpit chair and caught up on her email while she ate. Nearly all of the head librarians of the other forty-seven intersections' central libraries had replied, and each of them had said roughly the same thing—please send us your citizenship registration so that we can help you make an account, and then you can browse our digital archives and download whatever you want. No help there.

She had one library's worth of books, but Martin had

insisted that many more lived in storage, and there were all the other libraries just in Intersection Thirteen to consider. At the rate things were going, how long would she be able to gain access to them? And she had been lucky not to run into any problems with the staff today. What if she were not so lucky at other, smaller libraries where her behaviors would stand out much more prominently?

Damn it all. How could a civilization come to possess one of the most complete collections of the great literature of multiple Earths and then fail to care about it? It made no sense.

At that thought, she decided to see what *did* garner so much attention, if Plato and Cicero couldn't manage to command any. She logged into the Central Library website with Martin's credentials and was struck immediately by a large banner advertisement for 'New and Popular' books. She fought back her learned anathema for advertisements and tapped the ad. She was taken to a list of books, the top entry titled *The Everyone War*.

Mira downloaded and began reading. During the first five pages, she found herself laughing. The next twenty had her in stitches, but then her amusement waned. As the pages went on, she found her smile fading. On page 112, she realized what it was she was holding in her hands. She turned off her handheld computer, and exhaustion overtook her in a wave. Her eyelids grew heavy, and she found herself curling up in her cockpit chair.

Mira closed her eyes. "Everything still good with that computer program, Aurie?"

"Yes, Mira."

"Thank you, Aurie. Lights, please."

The cabin lights dimmed. Mira retracted her chair until it was completely flat and fell immediately to sleep.

Once, shortly after joining the Reconstructionists, Mira

had happened into the hangar bay for the metaxic ships, which was part of the Reconstructionists' secret hideout in the large hills near Granite Lake. Arn's father had designed and constructed it. Not only was it a hangar for metaxic ships, but also one of the hubs of their database of literature. They maintained hubs throughout the Hegemony's northwest, one of the primary benefits of the country's sheer size was the ability to easily hide things, even large things, away from government eyes—and even their drones' scanners.

When Mira had entered the hangar that day, she had not yet known Zekk well. He stood at a desk against the wall, typing away, the lines of code on his screen completely inscrutable to Mira.

She walked up to one of the four ships in the hangar (a fifth spot lay vacant; Trent was currently on a mission) and began walking around it, inspecting its shape, its details.

"Hello," Zekk called out.

Mira turned, but Zekk was still facing his computer.

"Hi," Mira said cautiously. She wondered if she should leave, so as not to distract him from his code.

"I'll be just a minute," Zekk added, and continued typing. Some moments and many keystrokes later, Zekk turned around.

"Mira, right?"

"Yes. Sorry to interrupt you. I was just curious about the ships."

Zekk smiled. "They're beautiful, aren't they?"

"I was thinking that. I love the way they shimmer when your perspective moves."

"That's the result of being exposed to the metaxia for so long."

"I hope that doesn't happen to people."

Zekk shook his head and let out a short laugh. "No. People never get exposed to the metaxia. That wouldn't end well for them. Sorry, I should have introduced myself. I'm Zekk."

"Nice to meet you." She shook his hand.

"Likewise. I read the copy of *Brave New World* you brought with you. Wonderful to have the original finally. When we got our hands on our first alt-copy, it was called *The Life and Times of a New Mexico Native*. That was a universe where Huxley wasn't a very good writer. We had a long debate over whether to even include him in the library. *Brave New World* is many orders of magnitude better."

"I enjoyed it, too. There's so much here to learn. I feel as though I could spend my whole life catching up."

Zekk gave her a sad sort of smile. "It won't take a lifetime. Enjoy this part while it lasts."

"Are you programming something for the ships?" Mira asked.

"Just working on the engines. That's most of what I do."

"So that we can outrun the Hegemony?"

Zekk nodded.

"How did you learn to do all this?"

Zekk shrugged. "I've just always liked this stuff. Coding is kind of like putting together a puzzle. You keep moving pieces around, trying different things, and the compiler yells at you throughout. Even when you can get it to cooperate, half the time the program doesn't behave the way you expect."

"Sounds frustrating."

"Sometimes. … Most of the time, probably. But then there are those moments where, after everything has been failing for hours on end, you find the way to make it work. It makes it all worth it."

"What's this ship called?" Mira said, pointing to the newest and most pristine metaxic ship, the one she was standing beside.

"That's the Liberalis."

Mira's Latin wasn't yet very good. "Liberalism?"

"Not exactly," Zekk said. "That word got corrupted in the twentieth century, associated with laissez-faire economic policies and social over-permissiveness. 'Liberalis' is much older. It's a descriptor for a person who acts like the nobility is supposed to, noble in spirit, even though they aren't part of any hereditary monarchy's family tree."

"A free spirit, then," Mira said, having just recently learned the meaning of 'free' as in 'above one's internal vices' rather than 'able to indulge one's internal vices.'

Zekk nodded slowly. "Yes. It sounds like you understand 'free' correctly."

Mira nodded. "Thank you, Zekk. Sorry to bother you."

"No problem. Stop by anytime."

Mira retreated from the hangar and returned to the base's library where she resumed her studies. She hadn't possessed the slightest inkling at the time that she might pilot a metaxic ship. Loving the books she'd discovered, she'd imagined herself working on the archive that stored them, thinking that one day the inscrutable code might make sense to her.

But even at that time, she'd felt a kind of connection. Something had drawn her to the Liberalis. Whether it was the ship's sleek design, or merely the idea suggested by its name—being noble in thought, word, and deed despite lacking any hereditary or economic advantage—something about the ship appealed to her even then.

When Arn had finally suggested to her, months later, that she try piloting, she had insisted on the Liberalis. She had never piloted any of the Reconstructionists' other ships. Not even once.

-28

Dear Arn,

Sorry for not writing to you last night. I was completely exhausted yesterday when I got back to the Liberalis and I just crashed.

The short version is that the damage done by the metaxic eddy is getting worse. Some calculations I did yesterday morning were particularly worrisome. It looks like the UMI wouldn't be able to evacuate all of its citizens in time if the effect is progressing at an exponential rate, which it seems to be based on this morning's numbers.

A government edict has been issued. About half of Intersection Thirteen's internal space has been declared off-limits, and everyone is to evacuate into their homes and shelters. They say that they can keep unaffected areas from receiving intrusions, so they're moving everyone into unaffected space and reinforcing them with potentia.

That's producing a lot of chaos for them politically. They've had to shut down most businesses and force everyone to stay home. Some people can work from home on their computers, but most can't. And with potentia being redirected to just maintaining the stable sections, there's nothing left to bolster people who were living on the edge, and apparently that's most of the population. I've read that most people don't have any kind of savings, or even possessions stashed away, like we do on Earth. It's funny. If I found myself living in a place where I could safely earn more money than I could spend and if I could trust the police and banks, the first thing I would do is establish a huge nest egg. I wouldn't blow every paycheck.

I know you're probably thinking I should get the hell out of here, but I want to stay. First, I've got Aurie set to get me out of here if the ship is in any danger from the intrusions. So far, they haven't affected the hangar bay and it's one of the reinforced areas, so I'm good on that front. Second, they still have so many books here. I scanned everything on the racks in their Central Library, but I've learned that most of their books aren't even on the shelves but rather in storage somewhere. The Central Library is now in a restricted section, but if I can find a way in, I might be able to get into the storage area and scan what's there.

I was able to get you a surprise, too. Can't wait to see you again. I promise to stay safe.

Love,
Mira

Mira stood over her backpack, which sat on the cockpit chair. It was mostly empty, but she'd stashed her computer and some ration bars inside. She wouldn't need anything else. She wanted to save as much room as possible for books.

She pondered how the day would go, all the challenges she might face in what she was planning to do. She kept coming around to the conclusion that the computer was her best bet. If there were armed guards or militia, she would have to evade them. She would use the light refraction program Zekk had made, which would render her mostly invisible, but the UMI was at least as technologically advanced as Earth was. She could be caught. Even in that case, she had programmed Aurie to fly back to their secret base near Granite Lake on Earth if she didn't return before the end of the day.

Even if they jailed her, Earth would still get the books she had managed to scan so far.

She reached for the zippers of her backpack, and then stopped mid-air as a thought struck her—a question that had been nagging her since she got here. But who could she ask? Martin came immediately to mind. She didn't have to give up any details, and it would give her a chance to find out how he was doing. That would give her some reassurance. She thought of Arn just then, too. She reminded herself of her promise to him. She also reminded herself that Martin was the closest thing she had here to an ally. Cathy and the senators couldn't be trusted at all. Martin... maybe.

"Aurie, establish an audio call to Martin Venner. His contact info is in my handheld."

A foreign dial tone erupted from the ship's speakers.

"Hello?" Martin's voice.

"It's me. Mira."

"Good morning!"

"Good morning. I hope this isn't too early."

"No. I'm up. How are you?"

"Pretty good."

"Will you be leaving?"

"Not quite yet. I'm still reading. Thank you again, for yesterday."

"No problem. It was my pleasure. I take it you've seen the news?"

"I have."

"You've arrived in completely unprecedented times. I promise it's normally much more laid back around here."

"I've gotten that impression. I wanted to ask you about something."

"Shoot."

"Something that crossed my mind. I haven't seen any mention of it in the media. Perhaps it's just ridiculously obvious to everyone or something. Anyway, I assume the Intersection has reached out to the metaxic organisms, right?"

"Metaxic organisms?"

Mira laughed a bit. Martin remained silent over the line. Mira stopped laughing. "You are joking, right?"

"No. What's a metaxic organism?"

Mira blinked a few times. "They look like blue blobs that form into people and they choose names based on nouns from some ancient language on your world. When someone on your world is about to enter the metaxia for the first time they show up and tell you about the travel restrictions. ... Martin?"

His voice sounded low. "I have never heard of metaxic organisms. No one has ever talked about such a species here."

"But... they're everywhere. They live *in* the metaxia."

"I'll see what I can find out," Martin's voice had grown somber.

For the first time since Mira had arrived in the UMI, she got the dark twinge, the twinge that happened when you worried if a Hegemony official had discovered something you did that you should not have done in their eyes, the feeling of wondering if their surveillance nanites were crawling on your skin despite your defensive programs, that habitual jaw-locking fear, the fear that screamed in the back of your mind for you to run, run, run to anywhere, away, to safety, somewhere closed, dark, hidden, and covered with a nice, thick blanket of anti-nanogenic EM pulses.

"Martin," Mira tried. "I've told you what kind of place I come from and what they do if they sense danger. It might be best if you don't bring this up... to anyone."

"Maybe you're right," Martin said. She didn't believe him. Something in his voice.

"We should talk more. Is there anywhere public we can meet, perhaps this evening?"

His voice lightened a bit. "As you can imagine, *Golden Circle* has been sealed in a quarantine field. And the government has ordered all the restaurants closed. I think the bridge where we met might still be... Yes, Darnem Bridge is open. Would you like to meet there?"

"Sounds good. See you at five?"

"See you then."

Mira ended the call. A country contained within a metaxic contortion, and its people didn't know anything about metaxic organisms. Mira shook her head. She would bet the Liberalis, though, that someone here did.

Main Street was even emptier than it had been the day before.

The other unsettling element was that the outlines of the spaces that had experienced intrusions had become encased in a shimmering, prickly void that seemed to absorb all light and made the facade difficult to discern. As she passed, Mira counted the affected structures. She had arrived at three when she came to her former apartment building as the fourth. *Golden Circle* was the fifth.

She hurried down the street and came to the gateway onto New Horizon Street. The gateway itself was abuzz with the shimmering black. Mira stopped and looked at the gateway in despair. She was nearly ready to turn around go back to the hangar when she noticed a woman moving toward the gateway and not slowing down. The woman walked confidently up to and through the black haze.

Mira blinked a few times. Had her eyes deceived her? No, a pair of men from further down the street approached the gateway and also passed right through it.

What was going on here? Had she read incorrectly? She thought the areas were restricted. She couldn't see any police or military. What was going on?

She decided, since it seemed completely normal to pass through the barrier and into the quarantine zone, to try doing so herself. She strode up to it, coming closer. She found she wasn't breathing. Her whole body was rigid. She was probably moving mechanically, which would look strange, and so she forced herself to try to move more naturally.

The black haze was now less than a meter in front of her. A gentle buzzing sound filled her ears, grew louder, and she was through. She looked over her shoulder, and the black haze was behind her now. She was on New Horizon Street, and to her amazement, there were just as many people moving about here as on Main Street. What was going on? What was the point of quarantining particular spaces if people were free to move about?

She shook her head, deciding not to waste too much effort figuring out the social intricacies of this increasingly unusual culture. She had great works of literature to reconstruct.

There were more intrusions here than on Main Street, and none of the intrusions here were covered in the black haze. Mira even spotted an intrusion forming near an existing one. It was the first time she'd seen one in the process of expansion. It bulged slowly outward like an inflating balloon. No one moving about seemed particularly concerned about them. She decided to simply hurry onward.

Mira arrived at the Central Library and noted that it indeed was shut down. Even if people were freely moving about the street and entering adjacent spaces, none of them seemed to be going into the library. Large exterior windows showed a dark lobby with no people in sight. A holographic sign announcing the library's closure hung suspended in the air before the entrance.

Mira walked as casually as she could into the space between the library facade and the adjacent wall. Once she was behind one of the large tubes of the helix, she looked behind her to see if she'd been followed. Her eye caught a movement above her, and she looked up to see the wall push itself outward into a bubble. Her breath caught in her throat and she stared at it transfixed for what seemed like minutes but could not have been more than ten or fifteen seconds. The bulge ceased growing when it had reached roughly the size of Mira's head. Her heart was beating a million miles a minute, but she watched it carefully until she confirmed it had stopped growing.

She forced attention away from the intrusions and glanced about. No one had followed her, which was good, but she her presence here was decidedly conspicuous. Now, where would an entrance to the storage area be? Nothing obvious lay at the base of this strand of the helix. How about the other? She looked down to the other side of the structure. Yes. There was a door in the base of the other strand and there were no intrusions around it. She checked around herself again for people—still no one—and walked calmly through the center of the double helix. When she reached the door and was safely concealed from sight behind the other helix strand, she took off her backpack and retrieved her computer.

Within minutes, Zekk's programs had granted her access to the library's security console. She hit the "unlock storage entrance" button, and the door before her buzzed. She pulled it open and slid inside. She descended a flight of stairs into the pitch blackness of a windowless room. Concerned, she went back to her computer and continued poking around the console until she found the lighting controls. Nanite lumens erupted to reveal a room packed with rows upon rows of shelves containing cardboard boxes. Mira scanned the room's walls and ceiling. No intrusions that she could see. The stairwell was a concern though. It was narrow. If an intrusion happened there, she would be in trouble.

Was this worth it? She decided that it was.

She moved about the cool, dry cellar, pulling down boxes at random and ransacking their contents. Having established that a box did not contain what she was looking for, she left them open on the floor, their contents strewn about its base. It took her until lunchtime to find the archived classics. Once she had done so, she stopped glancing every so often toward the exit and just focused on the scanning. Before she knew it, she looked at the clock and found it was already 4:51. She cursed and stashed her computer into her bag. She also grabbed up eight of the nearest books, some Plutarch, some Augustine, some Spinoza, and stuffed them into her bag. She didn't have time to pick and choose.

At just that moment, she remembered something else she had seen that day, something that had only mildly piqued her interest at the time, but now she was thinking about her imminent meeting with Martin and what had happened this morning. She decided she needed some instruction in UMI history. How had a country occupying a pocket universe in the metaxia gotten away with never meeting the metaxic organisms? Even the most ignorant Hegemony citizens knew what metaxic organisms were. Sure, they also told themselves a lot of nonsense about the organisms being an arm of the Hegemony Secret Police, but they at least knew *of* them.

Mira moved to a box she had unpacked earlier and picked up two books, one called *The Founders: A Pictographic History of the United Metaxic Intersections* and another, more academic looking one, *The History of the United Metaxic Intersections: Bicentennial Edition.* She stuffed them both into her backpack and threw it on. She approached the stairwell, and—

Mira gulped. An intrusion had formed in the stairwell. It was only about the size of her head. She could pass it. And she did, scurrying up the stairs, but she would not be returning here. She hurried out the door, used her computer to lock it and turn off the interior lights, then hurried away, anxious to get back behind the protection of the black haze.

Martin was already standing on the bridge when she hurried onto it. He stood, leaning into the railing and wearing a dour expression. He brightened somewhat as Mira approached.

"Liberating more literature?" Martin let flash a brief grin.

"Perhaps," Mira said. "How are you doing?"

"Everyone's working from their homes. They're letting people go into the office and pick up their things, but they've emptied it completely. There's a cluster of intrusions in the break room. I haven't seen it, but Julia said that they've obliterated one of the cabinets. At least everything is fine here."

"Is it?" Mira asked.

"As long as the potentia keeps flowing, and the Gyrospire is back to full production. Should buy us time to figure out how to patch this up."

"I hope so," Mira said.

"I've been doing some other digging."

"Martin—"

"There are some scattered reports. An immigration officer was approached by a man who 'blobbed out of blue' while inspecting the situation of a minority group on a parallel world. He filed a report, and there was some media coverage on it, but then it was triple classified and he disappeared—"

"Martin, stop. This— Leave this alone, please. I'm sorry I mentioned it to you. I had no idea."

"I'm glad you did."

"Maybe you don't understand how this works. When people in power want something like this buried, you don't just go digging—"

"Not here!"

Mira looked into Martin's eyes. There was an intensity there, something she might even describe as a kind of passion.

Martin seemed to calm, and he dropped the volume of his voice when he spoke again. "Mira, from what you've described, you don't have a free press on Earth. But here, we do. Or we're supposed to be, anyway, even if there are people who insist on calling us names and diminishing what we do. What matters is that we find the truth, and we tell the truth. Nothing is supposed to be out of bounds. Nothing. Our society only functions if everyone knows the truth."

Mira wasn't sure how to respond. Deep in her own heart, she dreaded the idea of information being free to all. Everything in her experience had taught her that the really important ideas needed to be hidden away, kept safe and secret for those who knew how to use them without inflicting the twin disasters that the Hegemony and Equum represented. Both Plato and her own life experience had taught her as much.

"Be careful," Mira said.

"I will. I'll let you know what I find. Do you have more reading ahead of you tonight?"

Mira nodded. "I want to learn more about your history. There was an alternate world Cathy mentioned, Isallna. It's where the Founders came from, right?"

Martin nodded glumly. "You're not fond of the Founders? I thought people looked up to them."

"Some people," Martin said. "I give them credit for the innovation of inventing metaxic contortion technology. They were also ruthless. Not to mention hypocritical. They were vocal about how poorly they were treated on Isallna, but the moment they got their own country, they did all the same stuff they said was done to them. You know that economic divide I was telling you about earlier?"

"It's all those of Isallnan descent who are rich, isn't it?"

Martin nodded. Mira held back a smirk. Some things didn't change no matter how many metaxic kilodivs she traveled from home.

"I can send you some stuff on our history, if you'd like. The less biased stuff."

Mira nodded. "That would be great. Thank you, Martin."

"You'll let me know if you learn anything?"

"I will."

"And you really don't know any physicists or scientific experts?"

"I don't, no. I thought you said the intrusions were contained."

"They are. But I'm still worried. Perhaps you haven't seen the piece we ran today. It's a projection of what would happen if we had to evacuate the intersections. The rich are already taking off for their second homes in natural universes."

She recalled there had been some ships taking off out of the hangar bay this morning, but she hadn't thought anything of it.

"Someone will figure something out."

"I hope so. Take care, Mira."

"You too. Something we say on Earth: watch your back."

"I will."

Martin smiled, waved, and headed down the bridge to the Darnem Street exit.

By the time Mira reached the Liberalis and was climbing up its ladder, she had grown thoroughly weary of the heavy books weighing down her back.

She clambered through the airlock, threw the backpack down by the lockers, and called out for Aurie. The lights came on.

"Hello, Mira," said a female human voice.

Mira shouted and jumped back against the wall, panting. The cockpit chair swiveled around, and in it sat Cathy, who now wore a black uniform with black gloves. Gone was the light tan formal dress she had worn the other day, similar to all the other UMI bureaucrats.

Mira panted and gasped for breath. "Hello," she managed between gulps for air. Damn it all. She had told Aurie to alert her for nanites or structural integrity breaches, but not for humans entering. Computers were so annoyingly literal. "You're not… with public relations… are you?"

Cathy smiled in a way that made Mira shiver. "In a sense I am. But not in the sense you first thought, no."

"If you were able to get in here, why didn't you just hack my computer and take everything you needed?"

Cathy's smile dropped to a harsh frown. "We are *not* like your Hegemony."

"You did break in."

Cathy's expression grew harsh. "Really? Would you like to expand our discussion about 'breaking in?' We could include the contents of your bag and what you've been up to all day. That's right. I didn't think so."

"I will make you copies if you want them back. But you stuffed them in flimsy boxes in a dark storage room. Didn't seem like you cared about them."

"What we do with them is our concern."

"I'm sorry," Mira said. "I didn't come here to cause problems for you. I just want to restore my world's literature."

"Speaking of that." Cathy put her hands together and made an arch with her fingers. "We have no quarrel with your… literary interests. We were prepared to ignore your adventure today. However, we strongly advise, for the duration of your visit here, that you do not mention the metaxic organisms to anyone else. We wish you had come to us with this information rather than going to our media."

"I thought everyone knew about them. Everyone who's been out in the metaxia, anyway."

"Not Intersection citizens."

"Except you."

"That's right."

"And your group is?"

Another awful smile. "We're called the Bureau." Cathy stood and moved toward the airlock.

"What will happen to Martin?"

"Nothing, as long as he gives up on his search."

Mira did her best to hide the fact that she was screaming at herself inside. "I see."

"If you have any more ideas about garnering outside assistance, please contact *me*."

"All right."

"Good night."

"Good night."

Cathy descended down and out the airlock.

As soon as she was gone, Mira ordered Aurie to re-encrypt everything, the entire computer system, including—she had to look up the thing Zekk had told her about—a full rotation of every security key in the system. She initiated the other programs Zekk had mentioned, the ones that rebuilt all the ship's nanites using the new security keys and disassembled all the old nanites, just in case they'd become compromised.

That done, she threw herself down in her cockpit and ran her hands across her face. What had she gotten herself into? The more time she spent here, the more it seemed that the UMI had not so much overcome authoritarian rule, as built a complex bureaucracy of supposed egalitarianism on top of it. She went to her backpack, picked out the textbook on the history of the UMI, sat back down in the cockpit, and began to read.

When Mira had been a small girl, her mother had kept her in the back of their store. Most days, her mother would pull up the computer after breakfast, and Mira would do the digital lessons until lunch. It was from these Hegemony training guides that she learned to read, to do basic mathematics, and also a form of history. In hindsight, she realized her mother had carefully planted critical thinking skills inside the lessons, encouraging her to analyze the texts and never take them completely at face value, even with those simple lessons.

In the afternoon, she would do the exercises on her own. Some days, her mother even let her play in the back yard behind the shop.

One day, when she'd finished her lessons, she asked to go into the back yard and continue working on the hole she'd been digging, but her mother told her she couldn't. She had to wait patiently until five.

Mira was put out. Why couldn't she go work on the hole? It was going to go all the way to the center of the Earth! And she'd discover things underground that no one had ever seen. She'd thought the grown-ups were being mean for no good reason.

"Mira." Her father appeared in the doorway to the front room. Mira had never been in the front room. It was off-limits. She'd glanced into it a few times when her father went in there, but that was the store, and Mira was never to go into the store.

"I want you to come in here."

Mira looked at her mother, who only nodded morosely.

Well, today, Mira realized, she would finally go into the front room.

Her father held the door open for her, and she stepped hesitantly inside. She found herself behind a counter, one whose surface was just a little higher than her head.

"Come through here." Her father held open a gate in the counter, and Mira passed through it, into the center of the room. All the walls were lined with shelves and each shelf was filled with boxes, vials, and bottles, ranging wildly in size and color.

"Do you know what we sell here?" her father asked.

"Medicine."

"That's right."

"Do you know why we have asked you to stay in the

back room?"

"Because there are bad people. That's what mom says."

"Most of the people who visit us aren't bad. But sometimes they are."

"Come back around here." Her father motioned back to the gate. She returned to the area behind the counter. Her father crouched down in the corner and flipped open a latch in the floor. Beneath the latch lay a button.

"You see how this latch just flips up when you press here, like this? It's so that you could do it with your foot. You could stand behind the counter, and no one would know you were doing it."

"What happens when you step on the button?" Mira whispered.

"A couple of things. All of our computers except for one will be wiped clean. A signal light, bright red, will go off in the back room, where you and mom spend most of your time."

"I've never seen it," Mira said.

Her father nodded. "That's right. But if you do, your mother will get the guns and point them through there." He pointed to a slot in the wall near where it met the ceiling, just to the right of the door into the back room.

"Because there would be bad people."

"Yes. Now, Mira, this part is very important. There is a certain kind of bad person. They are called the Hegemony militia. They wear dark, black visors that cover the top half of their faces and orange-yellow uniforms. If they come here wanting trouble, it will do no good to try to scare them off with guns or defend ourselves. If that ever happens, I need you and your mother to run, Mira."

"No! I wouldn't leave you, daddy. I wouldn't!"

"Mira." He grabbed her shoulders. "Please listen. If they come here for trouble, there is nothing your mother and I can do against them. Except get away. Do you understand?

The only way you would survive is to get away."

Tears had appeared at the edges of Mira's eyes. "Why would they do that, daddy? Why?"

Her father gulped, and the look of sadness upon his face was profound. "Because some of them are very greedy, Mira. And all of them are cruel. Your mother and I are doing the best we can to make sure you understand that you have a responsibility to be a good person. Not only to others, but primarily to yourself. The Hegemony soldiers... most of their parents teach them only to care about themselves. I know it's very sad and very frightening, but I need you to understand how all this works—"

"Why, daddy?" Mira stomped her foot and tears streamed down her face. "Why? There's a hole in the back yard and down below in the Earth are treasures and wonders no one has ever seen before, and up here we have to have guns and buttons for red lights because of evil people, why?"

"Because we also need to eat, Mira. And we need a warm place to sleep at night. And because one day..." He almost drifted off, his gaze darted away only momentarily, but then it returned, harder than ever. "Because one day your mother and I won't be here anymore, and it will be up to you to take care of yourself."

He pulled her close and hugged her tightly then, and she wrapped her arms around him. Her parents would not be there forever... The realization stung. It had stung even harder seven years later when Hegemony soldiers had indeed showed up, and they had wanted to take everything in the store and to pay nothing, and her mother had insisted on going out into the front room so that her father would not be holding his own against them, and Mira had tried to creep up to the door to try to hear what was being said and hadn't even gotten halfway there when she'd heard the shots.

She had almost collapsed, but she hadn't. Instead, she had remembered what her father had said that day and so many times in the seven years after. What to do if the Hegemony soldiers showed up. What to do if the red light went off, which it had, just before she'd heard the shots. Filled with rage, resentment, sorrow, all spilling out of her in a torrent that made her want to scream amongst the muffled sound of laughter and chest-thumping of the pigs who had just murdered her parents, somehow, deep inside her, Mira found herself just able to latch on to the promise she had made to her father. She grabbed up the backpack that remained sitting there, the one beside the back door, and she ran, out the backdoor, through her back yard, around the small, unfinished depression in the Earth that was supposed to have been her tunnel to the riches of the center of the Earth, and away into the Montana wilderness.

-27

Dear Arn,

The more I learn about the UMI, the weirder and more self-contradictory they become. Yesterday, I snuck into the storage area for their Central Library. I scanned as much ancient literature as I could, but also grabbed a few history books on my way out. I spent a good chunk of the evening reading up on them.

They seem to have two different versions of their history. First, what they have in common. Two hundred and seventy-nine years ago, a group of about a dozen men from a parallel Earth called Isallna got fed up with being treated as an underclass. They hijacked a bunch of metaxic ships and set out looking for a parallel Earth to call home. They found a suitable world straightaway but ran into a bunch of problems generating power and building out a civil infrastructure. One of the group, Marcus Stolten, decided to see if he could generate the power they needed by stabilizing a metaxic contortion. It worked so well that they abandoned the world they'd settled together and took up residence in the intersection itself. Pretty soon, others were duplicating his success and establishing their own intersections, and before long it was necessary to bring all of those into a unified political body.

Everyone agrees on all that. Where they differ is in the character of those original men, who they call the Founders.

To one group, the Founders represent a kind of mythical heroic archetype. All their modern political problems are interpreted as the failure of modern people to live up to the grand heights achieved by the Founders, most especially immigrants, who they perceive as wanting to mooch off the economic systems without adopting any of the values and beliefs of the mainstream culture.

To another group, the Founders are hypocrites. They think that the social and economic systems of potentia generation were explicitly constructed to favor descendants of the Founders and other Isallnans. The UMI is constantly seeking immigrants from other worlds, and they message themselves as egalitarian with a high standard of living, but this group sees that message as a lie, since the economic conditions of Isallnan descendants and non-Isallnan descendants are so different.

And there's something else. I casually mentioned to a journalist about the metaxic organisms, and it turned out he'd never heard of them. At all. No one here has. Except for Cathy. She's the government representative I met on my first full day here. But it turns out she's part of some secretive organization called the Bureau. She's warned me not to go telling anyone else.

So, here's my plan. First, I'm transmitting all the book scans to you with this message. I don't think I'll get any more chances at any books in the Intersections anytime soon. It's too bad because I'm sure I've only gathered up a fraction of what they possess. They aren't protecting their libraries from the incursions, and the incursions are happening faster all the time. It's becoming clear that they're on an exponential growth curve. They can keep unaffected areas stable though, so perhaps they can continue to hold the phenomenon off indefinitely. I suppose only time will tell.

I know you'll want me to come home, and I have to admit, the thought is tempting. But you know me. Now that I'm confronted with a mystery, I can't let it go. I'm going to go to Isallna and see what they know about metaxic organisms. They've got metaxic technology, so someone there should have run into them. It will also be good to learn what they think of the UMI, to get their perspective on things. Don't worry, I'll be super careful, as always.

And who knows, maybe Isallna will have more books.

Love,
Mira

Mira spent four hours piloting the Liberalis to a world on the far side of a metaxic sub-stratum adjacent to the one in which she'd discovered the UMI. When she arrived, she parked herself a few divs away from the world's metaxic coordinates and did a thing she wouldn't normally do—she broadcast a message announcing her presence and her desire to visit them.

These were, however, quite unusual circumstances. Having had her ship in Intersection Thirteen for almost a week, it was nearly impossible that Hegemony ships were still lurking nearby. They would have given up and returned to Earth long ago.

"My name is Mira Rous," she said. "I'm a metaxic explorer wishing to learn more about your culture and literature."

There was silence for many minutes. Mira worried that she would not be welcome, or worse, that the Isallnans were sizing up her defenses and planning how they could capture her ship. However, before too much longer, a voice erupted from her speakers.

"Hello? Mira Rous?"

"Speaking."

"This is Cecilia Reynolds, Prime Regent of the East Bremm Cooperative. We would be happy to receive you as a visitor. We're transmitting coordinates where you can park your ship."

"Thank you. I'm looking forward to meeting you."

Mira input the coordinates in the transmission from Cecilia, and the view from Liberalis monitors of the swirling blue metaxia peeled away into a field, a very large one of brown-red earth dotted with tufts of tall, lavender-hued grasses. In the distance on her left lay a forest, whose trees resembled morel mushrooms to her, their leaves splayed-out white stars. The grasses and shrubberies were purple, and the sky was a greenish-blue. Wispy white clouds drifted by overhead. To her right lay what looked like a village. All of the structures were constructed of white wood, nothing of metal. People moved about amongst them, and two of them, a man and a woman, were heading toward her ship. They looked an amicable and ordinary enough pair. Their clothing was much brighter and more done up than UMI clothing, but nothing frilly or ornate. The pair looked very practical. The man, in particular, was tall and, if Mira was honest, quite handsome. Looks, she reminded herself, had a way of deceiving.

Mira gave Aurie security instructions and hurried down out of the Liberalis's airlock.

The air smelled good, much fresher than the interior of Intersection Thirteen, which, Mira now realized, hadn't been stale so much as sterile. The sun was warm, and the gusts of wind felt good on her face, too.

The man and woman approached, and Mira faced them. The man and woman bowed, and Mira returned the gesture.

"Welcome to East Bremm," the woman said. "I'm Cecilia Reynolds. We spoke on the transmission. You must be Mira Rous."

"Just Mira will be fine. Thank you."

Cecilia gestured to the man. "This is Daniel Meyer, Senior Vice Regent for the Cooperative."

"Nice to meet you," Daniel said.

"Likewise," Mira nodded.

"May I ask how you found the coordinates for our particular Isallna?"

Good. Mira was glad to at least get that out of the way. If she wouldn't be welcome here over it, best to establish that now.

"Well," Mira said. "I downloaded the coordinates from the computers of the United Metaxic Intersections. Specifically, Intersection Thirteen."

"I see," Cecilia said.

"Are you a UMI citizen?" Daniel asked. He was trying not

to sound defensive, but Mira got a strong sense that the idea unnerved him.

Mira shook her head. "No. I'm from an Isallna much further away. It's called Earth. I was exploring when I stumbled across the UMI. I copy books. That's all."

Cecilia and Daniel both brightened. Cecilia continued. "We'd be happy to share with you what we have in exchange for the opportunity to learn about Earth. We can transfer digitally to you, if that would be acceptable."

"Of course!" Mira smiled.

"Well," Cecilia said. "Come with us, and we'll show you around the city."

Mira stashed her computer into her backpack and followed Cecilia and Daniel down the path toward the cluster of white structures in the distance. Light breezes blew at Cecilia's hair, and she held herself tall and stately. Her posture was excellent and all her movements seemed to be executed with precision. Daniel, on the other hand, walked in a much more carefree manner. He seemed to be almost glowing, maintaining a permanent, admiring smile for many moments whenever Mira caught his eye. Great. That was the last thing she needed.

"Do you have a large library of alternate literature on Earth?" Cecilia asked.

"It's a bit more complex than that," Mira said. "My society destroyed its literature. My group is reconstructing it."

"Won't other worlds' literature be different?" Daniel asked.

"Yes, but we have computer programs that can compare and contrast all the differences of many versions of the same text. In some cases, we believe we are very close to the Earth originals."

"So," Cecilia said, "each version you find brings you a little closer to yours."

"That's it exactly." Okay, time to learn something about them. "How do you feel about the UMI here?"

"I would call relations cordial, but not friendly," Cecilia said. "Many of the Cooperatives bar the UMI immigration teams from entering their territory."

"And yours?"

"We usually tolerate them. But there have been instances when they have been disruptive. In such instances, we ask them to leave."

"And have they?"

"Yes," Daniel said. A bit too quickly. Mira looked at Cecilia. She had a good poker face. If there was something more to such incidents, she covered it well.

They were getting closer to the city now, and the buildings were coming into better view. Many of them were multilevel, but nothing over eight or so stories tall. The tallest buildings were clustered near the edge of a large, pink-hued lake.

"That is the library." Cecilia pointed to the city's only stone structure, a six-story edifice with ornate carvings and tall windows of complex stain glass patterns, though they were too far to make out from this distance. "I'm afraid we don't have books from other worlds, but we have much of our own going back almost four thousand years. Daniel will take you there tomorrow."

"Thank you," Mira said. Perhaps she should take them at face value about the UMI. Perhaps she should let the UMI go, scan all the books and leave. Perhaps, it occurred to her, that she could also view this as another opportunity. Having been in the Intersection Thirteen hangar for five days, the Hegemony ships had completely lost track of her. She could travel to worlds unharried for once. But then she looked at Cecilia's face and at Martin's. She watched the people moving about the city of East Bremm. There was something about Isallna and the UMI. Something more that they weren't sharing. And, try as she might to refocus herself on her mission, it would bother Mira until she knew what that was.

They came to a long, two-story building at the edge of town. As they drew closer to its entrance, Mira saw that, even here at the city's periphery, numerous groups of people were milling about the streets. Mira found herself having a similar reaction to seeing so many people moving about in public as she had in the UMI—the oddity, from her perspective, of people moving about without any obvious signs of being in fear of others. What was different about Isallna was the character of that social movement. The UMI citizens had moved about with a kind of fervor, eager to get from one place to another. Even the groups she'd seen in the gardens, ostensibly not on business, moved around alone, with only one other friend or significant other, or at times a small family. Here Mira witnessed multiple groups of individuals talking amicably with one another, walking somewhere down the street, members of one group calling out to others, everywhere people fraternizing, no one in a particular hurry or moving in a single-minded, isolated way.

The novelty of a large society without fear had worn off, but everyone being so friendly? Novelty struck Mira all over again.

A group of young people stood in front of the building's double-doored entrance talking about plans for a farm as Cecilia led her inside. Mira was so busy eavesdropping that she almost missed what Cecilia said next.

"This is called a residence. It is mostly used by young people who have internships in East Bremm and are trying to decide if they would like citizenship here. I apologize for the simplicity of the arrangements, but it's the best we could do on short notice."

"Thank you," Mira said. "It's lovely."

"I must go now to attend to matters of state, but I hope you'll be able to join us for dinner."

"I'd be delighted."

Cecilia took her leave, while Daniel showed her to the front desk and helped Mira get checked in before excusing himself as well, explaining that he would come back in a little over two hours to take her to another building called the East Bremm Hall.

A young man, who Mira guessed was something like a bellhop, showed her up to her room, seeming surprised and a bit put off that she wanted to carry her own backpack. They walked up two flights of stairs, down a hallway, past many doors until they came to one halfway down the hall. He helped her key her palm to the entry pad, then showed her into the room.

It reminded Mira of the interior of a hotel, which she'd seen once in Boise, but with much nicer décor. The bed looked more comfortable than anything she had ever slept in, the windows had immaculate green curtains, and the furniture all looked new and expertly made.

The bellhop explained that clothes had been prepared for her in the wardrobe and then how the washroom worked. Mira marveled at the bathtub. A bath. She hadn't bathed since the first night in Intersection Thirteen, and that had only been the nanite decontam chamber in her apartment there.

She thanked the bellhop, who left still seeming put out, though she couldn't fathom why. She pondered it only momentarily after locking the door behind him. She went immediately back to the bathroom and gazed over the bathtub. She turned on the water to make sure it would be warm enough—success! Before too much longer, she had stripped down, got into the water, and luxuriated in the warmth. It seemed like only minutes had passed before her computer alarm went off, the one she'd set to make sure she didn't miss dinner. With a deep sigh, she pulled herself out of the bath.

She dried and went back to the small, adjacent bedroom, where she opened the wardrobe, pulled out the clothes they had left for her, and tried them on. They were a much better fit than the UMI clothes, and much brighter colors, too. All the same, she decided on something more staid, more dignified, hoping that the clothing would command more respect from her hosts.

Mira used the remaining minutes to look around their net, particularly the page for the library. It had all the typical promotional stuff—its four hundred year history, its dedication to knowledge in East Bremm, thanks to all its donors—Aha! Free access for educators, and here was the history section. Mira downloaded as much as she could. Oh, and the name of that Founder. She searched their general net for Marcus Stolten. What did the Isallans think of him? From a cursory glance, it seemed not very highly.

She got so engrossed in her reading that she almost missed the time. She packed up her things, which she refused to leave in the room unguarded, and took them with her out of the residence building. The sun had grown low in the sky and the twilight here set it aglow in purples and reds. Another interesting change was the presence of large insects, similarly shaped to moths, but with wing thickness and torso girth more like birds. They sat in clusters on the exterior windowsills of buildings. Every so often, a group of them would take off and flutter away somewhere else.

Daniel was waiting for her in front of the residence.

"Ready to go?"

Mira nodded.

"All freshened up?"

"Yes. Thank you for the clothes."

"It's nothing. They're very easy to make."

"It's interesting," Mira said. "I've seen a lot of high technology worlds. Most don't stick to wooden architecture like this. And I've seen more groups of people talking here than on others."

"As technology advances, some societies let it pull them apart from one another, atomize them. We resist that force."

"Then you have societal norms?"

"Oh, yes."

"And if someone doesn't like your particular norms?"

"They are free to apply for residency in a different cooperative."

"How many cooperatives are there on Isallna?"

"Over three thousand seven hundred."

Quite a few choices, it would seem. "Does that happen often?"

"With some regularity. About three percent of the population per year, but we gain just as much via immigration."

"How many emigrate to the UMI?"

Stony silence for a moment. "Less than one percent." He huffed. "The UMI is not exactly honest about conditions there, are they?"

"I wouldn't know. Do their recruiters lie?"

"They certainly exaggerate."

"What about?"

"The vast earning potential, the ability to remake a space into anything you can imagine, the ability to run a large potentia-generating firm. No one but a very few individuals from families who have been established there for generations will ever have even a small chance at such opportunities."

"But some young people latch onto the chance, don't they?"

Daniel seemed to consider his next words carefully. "In my opinion, it would be better for us to bar their recruiters from entering East Bremm."

"Does Cecilia agree?" The moment the words were out, Mira could tell from Daniel's face that she'd struck a nerve.

"Do all groups get along on Earth?" Daniel asked.

"No," Mira said, thinking of the constant tensions between the Hegemony and Equum. "Not at all."

"War?"

"No. Both sides are too technologically advanced. They'd obliterate each other. It's a kind of cold war. It's been that way for so long that it's faded into the background. No one thinks about it much unless they're trying to cross the borders."

"Here we are." Martin pointed to the doors of a single-story building, but this one possessed ornate wooden carvings. The lobby had beautiful carpeting, tall windows with silky curtains, and something like a chandelier suspended from the ceiling. Beyond the front desk were rows and rows of tables. People milled about everywhere, most talking in groups of two, three, or four, some already sitting at the long tables, all of them dressed up fairly well by Mira's reckoning. She was glad she'd chosen something more formal from the selection provided in her room.

Daniel showed her to a seat at a table at the head of the grand room, immediately next to where Cecilia already sat, and Mira took off her backpack, setting it at her side and taking the seat.

"How was the room?" Cecilia asked.

"Lovely," Mira replied. "Thank you."

"This is one of our traditions for visitors, a large meal. I hope you're hungry."

"I am."

People began to filter into their seats. Daniel took the seat on the other side of Cecilia, and a few minutes later, a bell sounded once, twice, then a third time. The hum of chatter diminished.

Cecilia stood. "We're dining today in honor of our guest, Mira Rous, from a parallel world where the planet is called Earth. She is a literature expert come to study and copy our books, and in this endeavor, she is most welcome here." The crowd applauded, and Mira stood and did her best to smile as well. She could feel her face grow red. Maybe receiving all this attention came easily to Cecilia and Daniel, but it did not to her. She'd spent most of her life trying to avoid any attention. She also caught a disturbing subtext in Cecilia's statement—welcome to their literature, probably not very welcome in digging into the UMI.

The food came out, served on their plates by men and women in blue and purple uniforms. Mira decided to keep the conversation light. Cecilia asked about Earth, of course, and Mira told them about the parts of Hegemony life that didn't involve goons and the parts of Equum life that didn't involve social avoidance, the latter based on her superficial understanding of how the Equum elite went about their day-to-day.

When they'd finished, Cecilia stood and declared that she welcomed warm relations between Earth and the Isallnan Collectives, and she hoped future relations with representatives from Earth could go as well as Mira's visit had so far. Everyone clapped again, much to Mira's embarrassment and discomfort, but she did her best to nod and smile, and then it was finally over.

The guests began to filter out of the great hall, and Cecilia excused herself. Daniel, on the other hand, stood and offered to walk her back to the residence. Mira accepted.

They exited into the night air. A breeze wafted in from over the lake, and the air smelled fresh, light, pleasant, but also exotic. Lights had come on atop posts in the streets, and they looked like nanite lumens. Mira would be very surprised if they'd been able to develop metaxic technology without nanotechnology, and she realized this was the first evidence she'd seen of nanites.

"Did you enjoy dinner?" Daniel asked.

"Yes, it was delicious. I'm sorry to impose. I didn't mean for you to go to all the trouble just for me."

"It's not an imposition. It's just how we treat guests. This is a very old Isallnan custom. It's in the classics, if I recall—treat your guests well, as one day it will be you on the road and in need of shelter, food, and rest."

Mira smiled. "Yes. Hints of it in Plato, and in the playwrights, too. Euripides, if I'm remembering correctly."

"We've taken that very seriously here."

"Thank you. I'll do what I can to return your kindness. Although, I'm afraid I can't recommend that any of you visit Earth."

"Oh? But your description to Cecilia—?"

"There were so many people. I told her only the good parts. The Hegemony will exploit any advantage they can find against you, and they will be ruthless in taking what they want. The Equum murders anyone who violates a moral and ethical code that shifts hourly. I'm happy to help you as a representative of the Reconstructionists, but our political power is somewhat limited." Mira let out a weak, uncomfortable laugh.

"How limited?"

"We are nine people."

"Ah. How do nine people hold out against the Hegemony and the Equum?"

Mira's sense of danger erupted to high alert. "We are good at hiding. And running."

"You must be very good."

"We get a lot of practice."

They came to the residence. "Good night, Mira."

"Good night, Daniel. Thank you again for the banquet."

She went up to her room, took off the clothes, hung them up, then crawled into bed with her computer. She spent the rest of the evening reading about the history of the UMI Founders from the perspective of the Isallnan collectives, and what she learned sent shivers down her spine. She composed a letter to Arn about it, and then tried to go to sleep, but found herself tossing and turning. She couldn't get it out of her head. She should have figured, though. Technologies that gave the good miraculous powers of creation also tended to give the bad devastating powers of destruction. If it were true, it was no surprise that the UMI had whitewashed that part of their history. Marcus Stolten had not started out aiming to invent the ability to sculpt spaces out of metaxic contortions. That was just a side effect of a technology premised on a somewhat more insidious proposition: the ability to unravel and obliterate quantum space-time—the metaxia—completely.

For a long time after escaping her home and the soldiers who had murdered her parents, Mira ran. She ran through the forests trying to follow the road that led north without getting too close to it.

"Go to Missoula," her father had told her repeatedly. "You'll follow the road, but not on the road. Move through the woods but watch the road. It will take longer, but it will be safer." She did just that.

The soldiers had come in the evening, and before long it was growing dark. Her parents had made other preparations for this event as well, and Mira grew more thankful by the hour as their foresight repeatedly paid off in her favor. The other thing her parents had drilled into her was to activate a particular nanite program in just this instance, which she'd done as soon as she'd gotten far enough outside Stevensville to feel safe. As the sun dropped below the mountains, a layer of nanites on her skin started generating heat.

Before long, she discovered another benefit of the nanite programs. She had huddled herself inside a hollowed-out tree stump and almost gotten to sleep when she heard rustling.

"Well, lookee here," a voice said, before she'd even had a chance to grab her bag.

She felt a hand touch her shoulder momentarily, and her whole body went rigid in terror, but then a sound like an electric bolt rung out, there was a puff of smoke, and the man retracted his hand.

"What the—?" His gritty, nasal voice now took an edge of anger. "Fucking bitch. Come 'eer!"

Mira tried to scoot into the interior wall of the trunk so that she could right herself. In the dark, she couldn't even see the man properly, and he'd turned some kind of flashlight on her, making him only a grim silhouette in the dark forest. She felt him pull her up and toward him, and then an even louder, almost deafening, electric roar erupted from her skin, then an enormous cloud of smoke.

The flashlight fell to the forest floor. Where it hit the man's leg, she could see that his pants were barely cinders, and the exposed flesh was brown with the texture of charcoal. Plumes of smoke were just barely visible, rising off his inert corpse. She thought he maybe twitched a bit, but perhaps that was just her imagination. She grabbed up her bag, and she continued running.

She was attacked just once more before she reached Missoula. That man had had enough sense not to touch her again after the first shock burned his hand.

Mira was now sixteen years old. She was so thankful for the nanite programs that her parents had had the good sense to prepare for this eventuality. She had no real idea at that time just how much money such software cost on the open market. She would not learn until many years later. At the time, she was just thankful for this last bit of their protection.

It was a few hours after the second attacker had been thwarted, in a copse outside of Lolo, the last township before Missoula, that Mira finally broke down. She had come out of the forests onto a precipice, the road off to her left and Missoula now visible in the morning light just beginning to peek over the Butte mountains. Before she had realized it, her face was wet; she was bawling and had crumpled to the ground.

Sixteen years, the vast majority of it with her parents in a small home that doubled as her parents' business. For sixteen years, she had had few concerns besides the worlds she had imagined into existence—the ones in the ground, the ones in the sky—and once she had learned about the metaxia, the ones that were right here and now but separated by quantum space. She had never wanted to leave her parents. It had been enough for her to dream up all those worlds and share them. She had listened to and heeded her father when he'd told her of the danger, but since it had never materialized, she had gone on believing that she would be able to go on living in that house indefinitely, that she would one day take over the store, and perhaps she might meet someone to run the store with her. That dream seemed, at that moment, as fanciful as the wildest things she had ever made up about the kingdoms underground and the civilizations in the air.

She lay on the cliff, and she wept. She was raw, spent in so many ways, physically and emotionally exhausted beyond anything she had experienced prior. She missed her parents. She missed them so badly, and how would she go on in Missoula, a foreign city that might as well have been London or New Delhi or Beijing. She thought briefly that she couldn't go on, but then the memories started flooding in—nights where her mother would tell her the stories from her own childhood, the days where her father had taught her how to stock the shelves, then how to run the register, then how to speak to customers, to learn to read them, to intuit their feelings, and help them find the right medicine, even when their symptoms were embarrassing or awkward to discuss. She remembered all of these things, and she realized that the gleaming sun was warm on her skin, the nanite program had stopped producing heat, her face had dried, and there was the city below her, the city her parents had told her to go to, where there were so many more people that she might just evade the Hegemony soldiers if they'd given up looking for the daughter they knew had gone missing from the store in Stevensville.

Mira picked herself up, grabbed up her bag, and began staking out a path down the cliff toward the city.

-26

Dear Arn,

There's so much to catch you up on. First, Isallna. It's not at all what I expected. I was expecting something closer to, but not as bad as the Hegemony. I realize now this was because the UMI citizens I've met are so insistent that their ancestors were escaping oppression. I'm not sure if all parts of Isallna are like East Bremm, or how much they've changed in the last three centuries, but there doesn't seem to be any oppression here now.

East Bremm is one of over three thousand "collectives," which, near as I can tell, is something akin to a city-state. They range from five hundred to about eighty-five hundred people each, meaning the overall population of this Earth is pretty small, but they are enormously productive. People who find they don't like the social norms in one collective are free to emigrate to any of the others, and there doesn't appear to be any social stigma for doing so.

The most frightening discovery is about Marcus Stolten, one of the UMI's Founders. An interesting tidbit that got left out of the UMI's history is that the technology he invented, the one that stabilized the metaxic contortion into inhabitable space, actually started out as a kind of weapon. The idea was to obliterate a universe from the metaxia entirely by destroying the metaxia around it, which would cause it to be subsumed into all of possibility. Pretty horrific. According to Isallnan history, he never used it that way, because he found he could make a ton of money off it by setting up the intersections. They paint him as a narcissist who gave up on his dreams of multiversal dominion when he discovered he could create his own dominion in the metaxia.

And that brings me to a deeper mystery, one that makes me feel worse the more I think about it. Everyone on every universe who has ever developed metaxic transport technology has run into the metaxic organisms. They show up right as you're about to leave, and they tell you something to the effect of, "It's fine for you to do this but be aware that the metaxia is our home. Don't mess it up." Well, I can't think of anything that would mess it up more than destroying chunks of it. So, that begs the question— why didn't the quantum organisms intervene to stop Marcus Stolten? What do they even think of the intersections? I presumed, when I first arrived there, that the organisms must have signed off on them because otherwise they surely would have stopped them from being created, but now I'm not so sure.

Another interesting detail. Isallna has some immigrants from the UMI, who, before that, lived on another parallel world entirely. Their story essentially goes like this: they lived a hard life on their original world; UMI recruiters show up promising glorious riches in the UMI; they emigrated and discovered that's a sham; they decided the best way to stick it to the UMI was to emigrate yet again, this time to Isallna.

These immigrants bring with them stories that puzzle and worry the Isallnans, namely, the fact that when the UMI recruiters showed up on their world and offered transport to the UMI, no metaxic organisms appeared. The first time these immigrants learned about the metaxic organisms was when they got exposed to Isallnan education programs. In other words, the metaxic organisms are explicitly avoiding the UMI, even when UMI citizens go to alternate Earths.

I get the feeling that I'm getting closer to one of those "dark things." If I were on Earth, this would be some piece of information that the Hegemony would not want me to have. I would flee. I find I don't want to do that this time. Perhaps I've spent too long running away. Or, perhaps I'm finally taking Aristotle's advice about right action. Either way, this is one mystery I'm having trouble running away from. Even though, I know, you'd tell me, this isn't my world. It's none of my business. I've gotten what books I can get from them. It's time for me to come home.

Except I can't do that, Arn. I love you and I miss you, but I need to know that this whole glorious meta-universe I live in isn't going to unravel around me or dissolve into a homogeneous expanse of all-possibility. Until I know more, I can't say with confidence that Earth is safe from the

UMI's weapons. They could know where Earth is now, and I would be responsible for that.

I'll get to the bottom of this one way or the other. It's time for me to stop running.

Love,
Mira

Around one-thirty in the morning, Mira decided she had turned over in her bed for the last time. She pulled herself up into a sitting position against the headboard, grabbed her computer from the bedside table, and turned on the lamp.

Her typical go-to in such moments would have, in the past, been Plato. On Earth, when she'd returned from a botched run—one in which the Hegemony had chased her off a world before she could collect their literature—she had gone to Plato for solace. His insistence on the existence of a perfect plane of existence, one where all that was perfectly good existed in pristine form, had been a comfort when it seemed that she and so many others were losing beauty forever at the hands of the mercilessly stupid and exorbitantly powerful.

However, she could not find her way into Plato that evening. She found herself skimming through other works instead and became ensnared in a large book she hadn't gotten around to yet, a partially reconstructed text called *Behemoth* by one Thomas Hobbes. After reading a few chapters, Mira checked the year of publication and recalled that it had been the age of the monarchies, those vast, powerful, hereditary feudal lords and ladies, who had insisted on the absolute obedience of all the others, called 'common' people—a social stratification that had taken centuries of work to unravel. Except that more than just the monarchies had ended up unraveling, it seemed.

Mira found herself pondering *Behemoth* that way. Hobbes's point seemed to be that the people had every right to disobey an unjust king, one who abandoned his duty of acting in the best interests of his entire country. But what, Mira wondered, would force those liberated people to act in anyone's best interests, most especially their own. One could see it all across the Hegemony—the majority of its citizens made choices completely at odds with their own best interests, let alone any higher concerns about ancient beauty or its preservation. They wanted entertainment and sensuality above even food, shelter, health, and safety. The Hegemony knew it, and they supplied the former in droves. There was no growing rebellion against their new monarchs. The Hegemony gave enough of the people what they wanted enough of the time that their less savory behaviors could be overlooked—such as murdering shopkeepers who refused to resupply soldiers for free.

All at once, Mira realized that the sun was gleaming against the window at the far side of her bedroom. She glanced at the clock and discovered it was already seven-thirty. She turned off her computer, got out of bed, bathed, dressed, and packed up her things.

The front lobby of the residence was busy that morning. At least a dozen groups of people stood milling about and chatting, some holding computers and going over the screens' contents. Deciding what to do today, perhaps? Mira wondered what the internships consisted of. At any rate, everywhere she turned here, she saw far more evidence of human collaboration than she had anywhere in Intersection Thirteen.

She found Daniel standing just outside the front door. He perked up when he spotted her. "Good morning."

"Good morning," Mira said.

"Are you hungry?"

"I could use some breakfast." The food would do her good, and especially coffee if they had anything like it. She was hitting that point in the morning where her lack of sleep the previous night had begun to dim her senses and muddle her thoughts. She knew from experience that it would eventually pass, but for the moment it was a minor burden.

Daniel took her to another community dining hall down the street, although this one was plainly decorated, unlike the ornate experience of the previous evening. Mira and Daniel stood in a queue, picked up individual dishes from a cafeteria-style buffet, placed them upon their respective trays, and then took open seats of no particular prominence in the center of the room.

"Community seems important here," Mira observed.

"It is," Daniel said. "Is it not like that on Earth?"

Mira shook her head. "It's mostly everyone for themselves. Except for the Reconstructionists. Literature brought us together."

"Nine people, you said."

"Yes."

"Why don't you do more recruiting?"

Mira's alerts went up, but she decided to test Daniel out a bit. "We have to be extremely careful. Literature and philosophy are both illegal."

Daniel looked at her with shock. "In both the Hegemony and Equum?"

"Just the Hegemony. But the Equum doesn't have any legitimate literature or philosophy. It all gets reshaped to match doctrine by the Grandees, the group entrusted to make sure no one is 'oppressed.'"

Mira watched Daniel carefully. He seemed almost sad. If he were planning how to use this information against her or Earth, he was covering it up very well.

124

Daniel finished what he was chewing. "And so, as a Reconstructionist, you have to hide what you are doing?"

Mira nodded.

"How did you get involved with them?"

Mira smiled. "Just some encouragement from my parents, and a friend."

She enjoyed telling the story. It was the most overt example of serendipity in her life.

Daniel shot her a smile. "That was very brave of you."

"I think..." Mira hesitated. She could sense what she was doing—opening up to him. She should not do that. She remembered Arn. But now Daniel sat here, looking at her with vaguely hurt eyes, wondering if he'd said something wrong. She decided to finish the sentence. "I think that it was mostly because of my parents. Before they died, they'd intimated to me throughout my lessons that there was something bigger and more important for human life than just food, shelter, and health. I figured that, if it was anywhere, it would be hidden somewhere in the ruins."

"It looks like you were right, if it led you to the Reconstructionists."

"I guess it seems that way."

After breakfast, Daniel took her to the library. It had large stone steps leading up to its entrance, and the stone columns at the front of its facade reminded Mira of the pictures of the Parthenon she had seen in restored books. The structure's interior reminded her of buildings she'd entered on her brief visit to the Equum city of Seattle. The shelves, desks, chairs, tables, lighting, ornamentation— everything—was impeccably maintained, and even though many people were moving about, it was very, very silent, unlike the Intersection Thirteen Central Library lobby, which had reminded her more of a train station until she had gotten into the stacks.

Daniel, in a hushed voice, introduced Mira to the library

staff. They quickly established what historical time frame and parts of the world Mira was interested in collecting literature from. Each and every such work turned out to be available in digital format, and by lunchtime, it had been prepared for direct download into her tablet computer.

They returned to the same cafeteria-style communal mess hall for lunch. The kitchen staff appeared to have changed, as had the menu. Besides that, the space held much the same atmosphere as it had at breakfast.

"Thank you for your literature," Mira said.

Daniel waved his hand. "It's nothing. If anything, it will help you understand us better. We have everything to gain and nothing to lose. It's the least we can do."

"I was surprised at Intersection Thirteen. They didn't seem to have anything from this period in digital format. Only paper books."

Daniel raised an eyebrow. "That does seem odd."

"At first I thought they must have been hiding it, but why would they, especially if they put the books out on the shelves easily enough."

Daniel seemed to think that over while chewing. A thought seemed to occur to him as he swallowed. "Did they have anything in digital format?"

Mira almost choked on her food. "Oh, yes. I had a look at that."

"Not very good, I take it?"

"No, I'm afraid not."

"Was it a contemporary writer you read?"

Mira puzzled over that momentarily. "You know, I'm not really sure. I went to their library's website to see what *was* available digitally, if not older literature. I just pulled up the most popular entry. If I'm completely honest, I was shocked at how bad the writing was."

"I suppose, based on what you described, you don't have any contemporary authors on Earth."

"Not of fiction, no."

"Time has a way of stripping away the fluff. A selection of contemporary literature is going to embody a wide range of quality."

"But couldn't you filter out the worst in the present?"

Daniel smirked. "How would you do that?"

Mira thought that over. "Perhaps a panel, maybe. You could get the experts together to judge new works before they're released to libraries."

Daniel was smiling wider. "It's been tried."

"And?"

"They're biased. Even the best. The shape of what they think is superior eventually becomes a kind of dogma. Works that contribute something new and unique are judged inferior for not meeting 'the standard.'"

"Then there's no value at all? Plato's *Republic* is just as good as *The Everyone War*?"

Daniel tilted his head.

"The book I read in Intersection Thirteen. The contemporary literature."

"Oh. I see. No. It's not that the two are equally good. It's that the situation is so much more complex. *Republic*—if we're talking about the same work, and I think we are—responded to and embodied an exploration of a core human desire, a yearning central to the human experience, and universal to all cultures and peoples throughout time and metaxic space. *The Everyone War* likely just wanted to make some quick cash by exploiting a popular ideology. It didn't contribute to anyone's development. It just told them what they wanted to hear."

Daniel and Mira entered into a long discussion about Plato, then Aristotle, finally coming around to *Behemoth*, which on Isallna, hadn't ever been written. It seemed that Earth and Isallna had fully diverged somewhere in the early Middle Ages. They had all the Romans and St.

Augustine, but no St. Thomas Aquinas.

After lunch, they walked outside into the street. Many citizens of East Bremm moved about the streets, nearly all carrying on some form of conversations in pairs or groups. Mira struggled amongst the throng to spot anyone going anywhere alone. It was a clear, warm day, and the sun shone brightly from the green sky.

"What will you do now?" Daniel asked.

"I'm going to search the metaxia for an expert in quantum physics."

"Oh?"

"I thought my trip here would provide me answers to the questions I had about Intersection Thirteen. Instead, I have more questions. They probably won't let me back in unless I bring such an expert with me."

Daniel seemed to ponder that for a moment, his gaze strayed away, and it set Mira on edge. She got the distinct vibe that his next words would be an attempt to play her need to his advantage. He turned his eyes directly to Mira's and said. "Would you be willing to stay just a little longer? I'd like to invite you to dinner with me and Cecilia at the Governor's Hall. It would be a private meal, but with Cecilia, too. The three of us."

Mira gulped and pondered that one over. Two instincts in her told her to flee. The first was a very old one, the one that jumped at any form of danger. The second was her thoughts of Arn. She should not head down this path.

Daniel dropped his voice. "Affairs of state are not conducted in public in any human culture I'm aware of."

"I see." That made her feel slightly better. He had an interest that wasn't romantic. Mira looked at the ground while she thought it over, then turned her head upward to look at Daniel again. No subterfuge, not that she could detect. He seemed far too sincere. He hadn't tried to flatter her, nor had he tried to threaten her. "I'll be there. What time?"

"Around six. Will you stay at the residence until then?"

"I'll go back to my ship, actually."

"Then I'll meet you there at five-thirty."

Mira nodded. "See you then."

As pleasant as her time in East Bremm had been (she had truly appreciated the bath), Mira found something even more comforting about returning to the cockpit of the Liberalis. She threw down her backpack onto the floor, clambered into her seat, and reclined it.

"Aurie?"

"Yes, Mira?"

"Activate the ANES. Start looking for metaxically aware worlds."

"How many candidates would you like?"

"Ten. Sort by overall technological rating. And I'll want to check the social indices, too." Those could rarely be trusted, but they would inform her level of caution, at least. "Dim the lights, too, please."

The cabin lighting and the monitor brightness diminished.

Mira yawned. "Wake me up at a quarter after five."

No sooner had Mira spoken the words than she fell into a deep and dreamless sleep. When the buzzer from her ship rang out, Mira felt as though she had only just drifted off. She inclined her cockpit chair and rubbed her eyes.

"You should know that a person is approaching the ship, Mira."

A shot of adrenaline surged through her and she was alert again. "Show me."

The large wall monitor brightened fully, causing Mira to squint.

"Oh." Mira deflated. "That's just Daniel. He's early."

Mira tried to smooth out the nice clothes she'd been

given as well as she could, brushed her hair a bit, just to make sure it wasn't completely frizzed out, then took up her backpack once more, and descended through the airlock.

"Good evening," Daniel called out.

"Good evening." Mira hit the ground and walked toward him. She hoped she didn't look too bleary from her nap. The sun was low in the sky, turning it a dark burgundy. The wind had picked up off the lake, and the mushroom-like trees rustled and waved their white leaves in the wind.

The two of them walked into the town, talking more about literature, Mira about the books she'd discovered on other worlds, the way the great authors had changed subtly over time. Daniel talked about the kind of writers they'd had in their own Medieval and Renaissance periods. They'd had a playwright of their own, a Shakespeare of sorts it seemed, around the same time but with a completely different oeuvre.

As Daniel was describing them, a thought struck her. She grew worried that she was getting too close to Daniel, leading him on. Her first instinct back at the library had been right, and this dinner was a terrible idea bound to blow up in her face.

Just as her attention came back to the conversation, Mira realized that they had slowed and turned before the entrance to a three-story structure with a gabled exterior, unique in East Bremm.

"This is the Governor's Hall," Daniel said. He held the door open for her, and she entered. She found herself in a space furnished similarly to the banquet hall the evening before, but instead of the large, long tables, flights of stairs and doors to adjacent rooms appeared before her. A man and woman wearing uniforms, some kind of guards, stood at the doorway. Daniel retrieved a card from his inside breast pocket and held it out. The guards moved silently aside.

Daniel led Mira up one of the flights of stairs, through a door, down a carpeted hallway, past many other doors, then finally to a door near the end. He knocked.

"Come in." The voice was muted by the door, but Mira recognized it as Cecilia's.

Daniel opened the door, and followed Mira inside. Before her lay a room lined with bookshelves in some places and adorned with paintings and busts in others. One of the busts bore an uncanny resemblance to Aristotle. At the center of the room was a circular table, where Cecilia already sat. A green tablecloth, delicately embroidered, lay atop it, and on top of that were three place settings, candles, and an assortment of trays covered with rounded, silver cloches. Cecilia promptly stood.

Daniel pulled out a chair for Mira, and she sat. He sat himself at the third place, and Cecilia sat back down.

Cecilia turned to Mira. "Did you find everything you were looking for today?"

"Yes," Mira replied. "Thank you. My computer is running everything through our comparison program. When I get back to Earth, we'll store everything in redundant backups."

Staff entered the room through a side door. One began pouring drinks, while another started removing the lids, revealing trays of steaming food.

"Do you read the originals as well as your reconstituted Earth versions?" Cecilia asked.

"Yes," Mira said. "It's informative. So are the authors we don't have. We've run into a number of works that we're certain were never written on Earth and are quite good. We collect those, too. I'm curious, you have metaxic technology, but only your own literature. Don't you collect also?"

"No," Cecilia said. She hadn't been curt, but Mira could tell from the very slight tension in her facial muscles that she had tried very hard not to be.

"We don't explore the metaxia anymore," Daniel added.

Mira decided not to pursue the topic any further and looked at the food on her plate.

"Mira." Cecilia's smile had returned. "Daniel tells me that you'll be looking for an expert in quantum physics."

Mira nodded. "That's right. It's the leverage I'll use to get back into the UMI."

"What do they want with an expert in quantum physics?" Daniel asked.

Mira decided to have a go at it. It wasn't as though it would remain a secret for long, anyway. Isallna would find out about the UMI's problems within days, if some cooperatives hadn't already. Mira explained to them about the metaxic eddy, about the metaxic intrusions, about the calculations she'd done, and about her experience in the library storage room. All those books, about to vanish.

"I just wanted the books at first," Mira said. "But it's become more than that. I need to know why the metaxic organisms avoid the UMI, and I read—" Mira paused and considered herself, then decided to plunge forward. "I read about Marcus Stolten. Your history of him. I learned about the weapon he created. I need to learn how to protect Earth from it, if I can."

Both Daniel and Cecilia were frowning now.

"Do you remember when you told me about the Hegemony and the Equum?" Daniel asked. "You called it a kind of cold war, created by the fact that both sides can ensure the other's destruction. Well, it's the same here. We never figured out how to protect ourselves from a Stolten bomb. We merely learned how to build them ourselves."

"Oh." Mira gulped.

Cecilia was looking at her inquisitively now. "And their books?" she asked. "Would you still save their country to get access to their literature?"

What a question. Mira chewed, swallowed, and set her silverware down. There was so much there. Yes, she wanted those books, but she was also afraid of what the UMI would do if she were to help them stop the metaxic intrusions. Would they repay her generosity with kindness, or would they go after her, or even Earth's universe, for learning the truth about Marcus Stolten and his weapon?

Mira nodded. "I want to get their books. I can transmit them back to Earth, even if I can never go back there myself." Saying the words stung. As horrible as the Hegemony and the Equum were, Earth *was* her home.

"How would you feel about me accompanying you back to Intersection Thirteen?" Daniel asked.

Mira looked into his eyes. He seemed quite serious.

"Before I took my position as a regent, I was a professor of physics at East Bremm University," Daniel added. "My specialty is metaxic studies. I have to admit, I'm more than a bit curious about this phenomenon of metaxic intrusions. It sounds as though the intersections' quantum scaffolding is deteriorating. We've always known that the eddies could cause damage, but we never imagined that the effect could be progressive."

Mira had to stop eating in order to take that all in. Could she really bring Daniel back to Intersection Thirteen with her?

"I would take my own ship, of course," Daniel added.

Mira continued to think through the possibilities, contingencies, all the potential ways this could go awry.

"If it's not acceptable to you, I will stay here."

"But..." Mira decided to say what was on her mind. "You just admitted you were curious."

"We respect your endeavor to restore the literature of your world." Cecilia placed her fork and knife down and looked directly at Mira. "Perhaps Isallna looks like a utopia to you, but I assure you it is not. We have our share of social problems, some of them quite taxing on our political and economic systems. But we struggle through. The effort that takes up most of our attention is making sure that the people on top have the best interests of *everyone* at heart. If I let Daniel interfere with your mission, I would not deserve my post as Prime Regent, and the other Regents would soon know it."

Mira couldn't believe what she was hearing. "You need to come, then. If only because I am genuinely worried about the lives of UMI citizens. I don't think I'd be able to look at myself in the mirror if the intersections ended up collapsing because I refused to let a scientist go there and investigate the intrusions."

Cecilia smiled. "I hope we will get to meet the other members of the Reconstructionists someday."

"I hope so, too." Mira meant the words, but she still wondered at her growing sense of trust. Every iota of her being told her to look for deception, for ulterior motives, for signs of a possible attack. Be ready for flight. Be ready! At any moment the dagger will come. But being deathly afraid of daggers was no way to live. Perhaps the Cooperatives had found a better way for people to live together than there had ever been on Earth. That was a big hope, but it seemed like one worth reaching for.

After dinner, Daniel offered to walk Mira to the residence. On the way back, she told him she was very grateful for the room, but she wondered if she might go back to her ship since she seemed to sleep better at the helm of the Liberalis.

Daniel let out a small laugh and walked her back to the field in which her ship sat.

"Where is your ship?" Mira asked.

"On the other side of town," Daniel said. "I can show you tomorrow. When would you like to get underway?"

"Whenever you're ready."

"Noon, then?"

"Sounds good. How many divs per hour can your ships do?"

"About seven thousand."

"Oh, good." She winked. "You'll be able to keep up." The words were out before she had caught herself. And, she realized, she had stayed out far too late. Was there even time left to write to Arn? She could sleep later, she supposed. Thanks to her nap, she wasn't particularly drowsy.

Daniel seemed to notice her smile drop. "I'll send my contact info to your computer system. Just message me in the morning if there's anything you need before we go."

"Thank you, Daniel."

Mira climbed up into the Liberalis, threw her backpack down onto the floor, herself down onto her cockpit chair, reclined it, and rubbed her hands over her face.

"Idiot," she told herself.

After a deep sigh, she groped around for her backpack, rummaged inside it for her computer, retrieved it, and got to work on her letter to Arn.

The days after teenage Mira arrived in Missoula became a blur in her memory. She recalled that she would go down into the market during the day and use the bargaining and people-reading skills she had learned from her parents to get herself enough food. At nights, she would find a park bench or some other such place to rest her eyes. There were a few more attackers, but the nanite programs from her parents continued to fend them off.

"Avoid the militia," her parents had told her. "They will possess stronger nanite programs than the ones in this computer."

She played their advice over and over in her mind,

heeding every bit of it as best she was able. More than once she had to run away into bushes or jump over a wall to avoid a patrol.

About a week after she had arrived, she found herself haggling with an older woman who ran a bread stall. After having managed to get a full loaf for half a package of bandages and vial of antiseptic solution (she had eight more in her bag), the woman had said, "there's another half loaf in it for you if you guard my stall from thieves." Then she whispered, "I've seen the sparks on your hands and the way you avoid touch when you trade with me and others. How much time is left on that program?"

The stallkeeper knew technology pretty well. Mira's parents had told her that they had purchased a license to run the programs for two years, after which they would deactivate. It was a mechanism to force the buyer to keep paying for the program's protection.

"Long enough," Mira whispered back.

Mira spent the rest of the day keeping guard around and behind the woman's stall. She managed to fend off a boy who thought he could pocket a roll without anyone noticing and an older woman who tried to surreptitiously, but much less gracefully, do the same.

"Come back tomorrow at eight," the woman said, "help me set up, and you can have a day's meal."

Mira had done just that. Over the next few weeks, she learned that the woman's name was Pelna, that her husband had died a few months prior, and that the stall was the only thing that allowed her to keep paying the property tax on her house. She had no children, and her neighbors kept her safe enough during the night, but running her business had grown progressively harder under the strain of thieves. The militia were, of course, no help at all. If anything, they were part of the problem—and that was the one problem that Pelna didn't expect Mira to help with. When soldiers showed up, Mira made herself instantly scarce, and Pelna never begrudged her this.

Mira held that job for just over a year. During those months, she came to know Pelna's regular customers well. One was a man named Enro, who often showed up together with a man named Hanith. They passed through Missoula often, either on the way to Spokane or just having arrived from there. At first, Mira thought they were just really good friends, but then, perhaps on the second or third time they showed up together, she realized their relationship was much deeper than that. Their interactions, she realized, were much more like her parents' than any friends'.

By this time, Pelna had offered Mira the side room in her house.

"Do you think that Enro and Hanith are ever in danger?" Mira had asked. "My parents taught me that if I ever found love, I shouldn't worry about whether the other person was a man or woman, but that if she was a woman, we would have to be extra careful about hostility from others."

Pelna nodded. "Your parents were very perceptive. But Enro and Hanith keep good company. I saw their comrades once. A man named Tirin from Spokane leads them and two others. He's a really good one. Kindhearted and strong. Seems honorable, too. You don't see that often these days."

"I think I remember Tirin," Mira said. "Does he have a son named Arn?"

Pelna nodded. "That'd be him."

"What does their group do?"

"They're traders," Pelna replied, but Mira got the impression that Pelna wasn't telling her the whole truth. As if to drive home the point, Pelna turned the topic of conversation to the bookkeeping for the stall, when the next property tax was due, and whether or not they'd have enough money to pay it. Mira had agreed to take care of the flour purchase the next day, since the stall would be slow on a Wednesday, and get everything prepared at home for Thursday's baking. Friday would be a big day.

But her curiosity latched onto Tirin. Pelna's reticence only made her want to know more than ever what he and his group were all about.

-25

Dear Arn,

I didn't find answers on Isallna, just more questions.

The UMI and Isallna both have the weapons I described yesterday. Isallna seems to possess them begrudgingly. It's their only defense against the UMI, it seems. There are no open hostilities, but neither are they particularly friendly, which explains why the UMI paints them as so oppressive without actually taking any action against them. In a sense, it's similar to how the Hegemony and the Equum treat each other.

Regardless, if I go back now, one or the other could track me back to Earth. I think now that the UMI was bluffing about knowing Earth's location. If both Isallna and the UMI have these "Stolten bombs," there would be no way to stop them from using them.

I'm heading back to Intersection Thirteen. A metaxic researcher from Isallna is going there, too. Hopefully, the UMI will have found a solution to the metaxic intrusions already. Either way, the goal now is not to get their books (although I will if I can), but simply to find out how we can keep Earth safe from their weapons. I refuse to believe that we now have to simply live in their shadow, our universe capable of being obliterated from the multicosm if one of them decides they don't like us anymore.

Who knows? Maybe Intersection Thirteen won't even let me back in. I should arrive there tomorrow evening. I'll be in touch.

Love,
Mira

Mira slept well that night. She fell asleep nestled into the cushions of her reclined cockpit chair. When had she transitioned to sleeping better in the Liberalis than anywhere else, she wondered as she drifted off to sleep.

Mira awoke to Aurie's voice, announcing it to be eight in the morning. It was only then that Mira wished she had not turned down the room at the residence, as a hot bath would have done her well.

Her stomach rumbled, and she alternated in her mind, ration packs or a message to Daniel. The former would taste like cardboard. The latter would risk more dialogue with a man she didn't want to get any closer to. But she did want to stay on Isallna's good side. That settled the matter. She messaged Daniel, and within minutes, he had offered to take her to breakfast, saying he would be there at the Liberalis at nine. He arrived promptly.

They went to the same mess hall they had yesterday.

"Do you expect you'll be able to help them?" Mira asked over breakfast.

"I'm not sure. We thought we understood the effect of metaxic eddies on artificial quantum spaces. It seems we don't."

"I hope they've started evacuating people."

Daniel nodded. "That would be prudent."

"Do you think that the Isallnan descendants would want to come back here?"

"I'm not sure. They're used to a very different kind of life. I expect they would see it as a burden to live here. Well, the rich, anyway."

"Why?"

"You can't sculpt out your spaces and make them into whatever you imagine. There are no large corporations to run. Our government requires its civil servants to uphold high ethical standards, not maximize potentia generation."

"It sounds like for most people it would be much better, though. Lots of people around all the time, friends and acquaintances everywhere, no need to worry about how much your next potentia drop is going to cover and all that. Right?"

"It depends. Even people in that situation might sense it as a loss of the *opportunity* to reach for those things that only the rich have access to. A lot of them believe that they can get there if they try hard enough, even though the reality is that they never will."

Mira frowned into her breakfast. The UMI seemed such a contradiction in terms. They possessed weapons of mass destruction they didn't use, and the largest collection of macrocosmic literature she had ever seen, without seeming to care that they owned it.

"What's on your mind?" Daniel asked.

"Just thinking about the UMI and a problem we have on Earth."

"What's that?"

"We call it the Great Silence. It's a period around the beginning of the twenty-first century when the voices of the last great writers and philosophers fell away. Something big seems to have happened in 2020 because the rest of the twenty-first century is a huge blank. Except for what the Hegemony and Equum tell us about it, none of which any thinking person believes, of course."

"And how does that relate to the UMI?"

"I was just thinking, the UMI has so much literature, but it's so hard to get access to it, and no one who lives there seems to care that they have it. What if what happened on Earth was like that? There was a reporter I talked to in Intersection Thirteen who suggested that perhaps the great thinkers didn't disappear so much as they got too busy. Everyone on the UMI runs around generating potentia and there's no room left for anything else. And that leads to what looks like a contradiction from the outside—they have this amazing legacy, but everyone's too busy to care that it exists."

"An interesting theory. Do you think there's any way to prove that something similar happened on Earth?"

Mira smirked. "Not unless we invent Wells' time machine. Sorry, non-overlapping literature."

"It reminds me of one of our writers though." Daniel described it, and indeed, the work sounded eerily familiar. It was funny how all the human themes ended up being described across the metaxia, each with different details, but the thematic cores never really changed.

After breakfast, Daniel took Mira to see his ship. It was about the same size as the Liberalis but lacked wings and a nose. It looked more like a large, oblong egg. Earth's metaxic ships had all been influenced by the fighter jet designs that were prevalent in the Hegemony. Since Zekk had been more interested in the engines than the hull, he had simply taken a Hegemony design and copied it. Daniel's egg-ship was painted bright yellow. Mira asked about the color.

"It clashes with everything here, sure, but it's designed to be visible in the metaxia against all that blue."

Afterward, Daniel walked her back to the Liberalis. As they approached the ship, Mira took a deep breath of the Isallnan air. This was the last genuine atmosphere she would breathe for quite some time.

"Take off at eleven?" Mira grabbed the ladder to the airlock.

Daniel nodded. "You bet."

"I'll see you at Intersection Thirteen, then."

"See you there."

When Mira clambered into the cockpit, she breathed a sigh of relief. She made a mental note to keep her distance from him when she got the UMI. He'd be off doing research somewhere, she was sure. Her first priority was to sync up with Martin, she decided. At that, her heart sunk. Martin. Ugh. Different person, same problem.

Mira threw herself into her cockpit chair. "Aurie."

"Yes, Mira?"

"Run all diagnostics and prepare the ship for an eleven o'clock departure. The destination will be Intersection Thirteen."

Mira passed the four-hour journey by having Aurie read segments of *Behemoth* to her while she flew the Liberalis. Every time he finished a section, she would glance out to her right to make sure that Daniel's ship was still where it was supposed to be. She did not contact Daniel, and he did not try to contact her. It was probably better that way. She suddenly wished she had grown up in a culture with a more robust sense of diplomacy. She'd spent her life avoiding everyone in power, and now suddenly she was supposed to mingle with them. She found it emotionally exhausting.

When the clock showed that she was twelve minutes away from the UMI, she began to notice movement in the distance.

"Aurie, those are ships, aren't they?"

"Yes. They are broadcasting UMI digital signatures."

Mira counted the ships as she approached, each one rippling and congealing into existence out of the same point in metaxic space. Five had appeared, then eight, then thirteen, each one shooting off in a different direction from the others. Most likely an evacuation. Mira supposed that meant that they hadn't found a solution to the problem.

Mira hailed Daniel's ship.

"Yes, Mira?"

"Should I contact them, or do you want to do it?"

"You have met them more recently. Go ahead."

Mira opened a communication channel to the Intersection Thirteen address Admiral Lake had used when Mira had first arrived. "This is Mira Rous of Earth. I'm here with Daniel Meyer of Isallna. He is an expert in quantum physics and metaxic mechanics. We're requesting permission to dock in the Intersection Thirteen hangar."

A minute passed, and then a voice rang out over the Liberalis speakers, which Mira immediately recognized as Cathy's. "Mira! Thank you for heeding our request. You and Daniel are welcome to dock. I'm transmitting authorization."

Mira wished very much that she had warned Daniel about Cathy, but there was nothing to be done about it now. She didn't dare do so over an open communication channel. Mira merely transmitted Daniel the docking coordinates, and both ships slowed to a crawl. The metaxic blue peeled away, and the Intersection Thirteen hangar faded into view. It looked much the same as Mira had left it almost three days ago, except that it was much busier and there were far fewer ships than there had been before.

Mira landed the Liberalis, then called up the mail interface and composed a quick message to Martin announcing that she was back and wanted to know when he would be free to chat. When she had hit the send button, she looked up and realized that Cathy and Senator Murray were standing outside her ship. Cathy was wearing her brown and green civil servant uniform, the same one she'd worn on the first day they'd met.

Mira climbed out of the Liberalis and discovered that Daniel had arrived there while she was in the airlock and was already introducing himself to them both.

"Good to meet you," Senator Murray said to Daniel as Mira approached. "We shouldn't waste any time. If you'll come with me." Daniel nodded to Mira, and he and the Senator took off toward the entrance to Main Street.

"How is everything?" Mira asked.

Cathy smiled in a way that made Mira nervous. "The fight against the degradation continues. We have had to restrict a few more sections, but everyone is holding up well. Most individuals have voluntarily confined themselves to their living spaces, working remotely as best they're able."

"Has the problem spread to previously unaffected areas?" Mira asked.

"Not exactly," Cathy said. "Our barriers can maintain the metaxic integrity of preserved spaces, but it requires a lot of potentia to keep those systems running. We had to free up potentia for other uses, and so it was necessary to let some additional spaces go. Nothing critical, of course. Founder Square, Main Street, and essential living spaces through all the Intersections remain stable. Thank you so much for bringing Dr. Meyer. What will you do now, Mira?"

Mira's warning sense twinged. She wasn't wanted. And she had a feeling she knew why. "I want to speak to Martin."

Cathy looked at Mira blankly for many moments, just smiling. "I see."

"I noticed ships leaving the UMI on my way in. Is there an evacuation?"

"Not exactly. Some citizens are choosing to relocate."

Those with the means, Mira thought. She hoped just then that the hangar was stable. It seemed to be. There wasn't an intrusion anywhere in sight.

Mira chose her next words carefully. "So, not a mass evacuation?"

"No, nothing like that. The situation is quite in hand."

"Well." Mira put on her best smile. "I suppose I'll return to my ship and await Martin's message." She walked back to her ship and grabbed the ladder.

"Mira?"

She turned. "Yes?"

"How many more metaxic ships do you have on Earth?"

"Five. Why?"

"Would it be possible to call them here? There's no need at the moment, but if it became necessary…"

"I'll see what I can do." Mira began climbing. "I'll let you know."

When she arrived in the cockpit, she had Aurie seal off the ship. No word from Martin on her computer, as she expected. Something had happened to him. She had read it on Cathy's face when she'd mentioned his name. Now she needed to know what had become of him.

"Aurie, what are the titles of Martin Venner's articles in *The Probability* over the last three days?"

"There are two articles. Published three days ago:

146

'Dangerous Times to Be Living on the Edge'. Published two days ago: 'Alone in the Metaxia.'"

"Nothing for yesterday?"

"There were no articles published by him yesterday in *The Probability*."

"Show me 'Alone in the Metaxia.'"

Mira pulled up her tablet computer and read. It was just as she suspected. He started with the broadly believed UMI truism that the metaxia was an empty space, devoid of anything but swirling blue, and then moved on to suggest that it would be possible for organisms to exist whose constituent being *were* quanta. Organisms, which, Mira knew, did exist. Martin had gone and revealed their existence to the whole UMI population. Cathy and her ilk must have loved that.

Guilt seeped in. Her fault. She was the one who had mentioned it to him. She felt wretched. She threw herself down in her pilot's chair, and she thought. She thought for quite some time.

"Alright," she said out loud, not really intending to. "Aurie?"

"Yes, Mira?"

"Search the UMI network for all references to Martin Venner in the last two days. And grab a copy of the most recent issue of *The Intersection Twenty-Four Post*."

If the UMI didn't want Martin, she'd get him out of here, but she had to find out what they'd done to him first. And she hoped, prayed, that his bluster about his government's progressiveness hadn't been completely unfounded. If he had been a Hegemony or an Equum citizen and done what he had done, he would have already been reduced to his component atoms and all records of his existence would have been purged from the official databases.

She sat down with her computer and started going through the material.

Eleven months after Mira began helping Pelna and five months after Pelna had invited Mira into her home, Pelna fell ill. Mira noticed right away when Pelna began wheezing and coughing. Pelna insisted everything was alright, but one day, a fit erupted while she was trying to work the stall, and Mira had to lay her down on the ground, then pack up all of the loaves and rolls and get her back to the house early. She drove Pelna home despite never having driven before. It was one of the most frightening trial-by-fire learning experiences of her life.

Mira cared for Pelna dutifully for two more months. Mira would bake all the bread early in the morning and tend to Pelna before packing up the truck. Then, she would go to the market and run the bread stall all day, come home and care for Pelna in the evening before getting four or five hours of sleep and beginning it all again.

"You are a gift from heaven," Pelna told her one evening, between wheezes.

"You took me in," Mira replied. "What kind of person would I be if I didn't help you through this?"

"You would be like most of them." Pelna jerked her head sharply toward the house's front door.

"Well, I guess I'm not like most of them, then."

"All the better. You would have gotten along well with Sal." That was her late husband. Pelna paused, looked at the floor pensively, then added, "And Rei."

"Who's—?"

"My son. He died."

"I'm sorry."

"Damned militia. Boy was far too bright. Head in the clouds, though. Went searching out contraband in the ruins, found it, got caught with it, no chance in hell to make the case he was planning to hand it over. An old story." Pelna had to pause for another coughing fit. Mira refilled

Pelna's glass of water and felt her forehead with the back of her hand. Not too bad, but perhaps a bit warm.

Pelna drank from the glass and then took a deep breath. "I beat myself up for a long time about that. Should I have discouraged him from running the ruins? Should I have molded him into a good merchant instead? For a long time, I thought the answer was yes. But not now."

"What changed your mind?"

"Because someone, somewhere in this world, has to care more about how we treat one another, how we live together, what it means to be good instead of bad. That's what he was chasing. He got it more from Sal than from me, but Sal wore me down with time. I came to see why they cared so much about it. It's noble. And not in that greased up, smarmy way, the way of being a president over people, of having power. No. The real way of nobility. The way that should command respect but doesn't, because most people can't even recognize it. Mira, my boy was chasing the same thing that Tirin and his crew are chasing." Another cough. "But don't you tell anyone that. I just thought you should know, so that—" Pelna was struck by another coughing fit, and Mira brought her more water. She tested Pelna's forehead again and now she was burning up. They decided to put their conversation on hold for the night.

Unfortunately, they weren't able to finish it. Pelna wheezed all through the next day, her fever raging. The morning after, on a frigid, bone-dry day in early January, Mira woke and found Pelna was breathing no longer. She knelt at Pelna's bedside for what seemed like an hour, weeping silently.

In the days that followed, Mira found broad support from her neighbors in arranging for a funeral and taking care of the house. A few days after the funeral, she began packing up her things, figuring she would need to move on and find a new place to live. She decided, before she left, to take one final look at all of Pelna's account books, just to make sure everything was in order, a safeguard against any surprise visits from Hegemony bureaucrats.

Pelna's financial paperwork just happened to include a copy of her will. To Mira's shock and amazement, she discovered that Pelna had left the house and all of her belongings, including the baking and stall equipment, to Mira. The alteration date was just three months prior.

It took Mira many minutes for that to sink in. She set down the documents and wondered how to proceed. Her brain eventually kicked into gear and she began to plan. Loathe as she was to enter a Hegemony government facility, she made an exception, just this once, to go the property administration office and apply for a copy of the property deed with her name on it. She hurried directly home thereafter.

By this time, she had a meager nine months left before the electrocution nanites that protected her would deactivate themselves. She had learned many things from Pelna in this time, and one of the most important lessons was that money meant power, and power meant the ability to protect oneself. She now had property, which was a kind of money, and she had gained her neighbors' respect via Pelna. Mira set about the work of learning more about each of her neighbors, bringing them offerings of bread, meeting their families, and finding out if there were any small ways she could help them out.

The plan worked. By the time the summer rolled around, Mira, only seventeen years old, had become owner and proprietor of a business, and she had a network of friends who lived around her, all of whom would rise to her support if she needed it and would notice if she went missing.

At night, Mira would sometimes lie awake and wonder

about her parents, if they would be proud of her or not. She believed so but she couldn't shake the feeling that something was still missing from her life. As she had become a young teenager, her parents, like Pelna in her final days, had started hinting at a world bigger than economics, a world that should command power and respect, but was now silent because of the Hegemony. What was that world? How could she get Tirin's attention and learn about it without scaring him away or worse?

As if an answer to her question, Enro showed up at her bread stall the next day.

"I've been thinking of expanding," Mira said as she handed over the bread.

"Oh?" Enro said.

"Yeah. I have some experience selling medicine, too, but I feel there's more out there, more I could do."

Enro shrugged. "Well, there's produce, dairy, textiles—"

"I was thinking of something more exotic." That was as far as she dared push, but she did want to push.

"Well." Enro shrugged again, trying to be nonchalant, but she caught the feint. "I suppose the most exciting kind of work around here is hunting relics. You know, all that stuff in the ruins." Small towns like Stevensville didn't have ruins, but Missoula did. An expanse of land outside the city core, which had once contained businesses, industries, homes, and all the rest, but which now lay dormant—the remains, it was thought, of the twenty-first century. Going there wasn't illegal, but lots of the stuff that could be found there was. Most avoided touching any of it, for fear it could be contraband. Some hunted it out anyway and sold it to the Hegemony to destroy, and for a hefty profit. But one needed to be sure enough of their social status that they wouldn't worry about the Hegemony turning around and accusing them of trying to own it, like what had happened to Rei. Mira certainly didn't fall into that category. But it was enough. Enro had supplied the hint. "But," he added, "you wouldn't be interested in that kind of work, I would imagine."

"No," Mira insisted, deciding to try her hand at injecting subtext. "You're right. Probably textiles would be more my thing. Or perhaps papermaking. I hear that's a lucrative profession."

-24

Dear Arn,

I'm back on Intersection Thirteen, and it seemed like they were doing fine at first, but that's just because the leaders are doing the best they can to project that they're in control. It's actually a complete mess.

When I left, they'd stabilized about half the internal area of each intersection, moved everyone into those areas, and given the rest up to the metaxic incursions. Well, from reading the news, every day since I've been gone, every intersection has given up more space to the incursions. The government line is that they are "freeing up potentia for other uses," but the phenomenon is so frequent and widespread that I wonder if they're being honest about *choosing to let sections go.*

There's something else I've discovered that, frankly, I'm at a loss to explain. I'm not sure you're even going to believe me. Before I left, I noticed that people were entering and leaving the supposedly "restricted" areas. I didn't think too much of it at the time, but after tonight's research, I've found the reason why.

Since I left for Isallna, the restrictions have been more stringently enforced. The people who were passing in and out before are some kind of subculture that believes that the incursions are "fake." That they don't exist. The thing is, I've seen one. In fact, I've seen clusters of them. I can tell you they're dangerous because I saw one eat up a part of a painting and another blow out a ceiling light in a cafe. However, this group thinks that the incursions don't exist, or, alternately, that they "aren't that bad." Some of them have even lost feet or fingers to expanding incursions and still insist that they should be allowed to move about freely. It's unreal.

And this isn't some fringe element. This is forty percent or more of the population.

Since I left, they've started rallying to petition the government to remove the restrictions, saying it violates their freedom. These people's idea of freedom couldn't be more different from ours, though it reminds me of something I read in Aristotle a few years back, how one of the ways democracies can kill themselves is by convincing citizens that their social institutions constitute a kind of tyranny. You remember the part I'm talking about, right?

Today I'm going to try to get my hands on more books. I'll

*also check in with the Isallnan scientist, Daniel, and see
how that's going. And, of course, I'm working on a way to
keep us safe from their weapons. Don't worry about me.
The Liberalis is in their hangar, and they wouldn't let that
section go because it's their only escape route.*

I'll write again soon.

Love,
Mira

Mira fell asleep thinking about her letter to Arn and woke
up thinking about her letter to Arn. It hadn't been a
complete falsification. If she found a way to access an
unaffected library, she would certainly take it. However, the
way the UMI government was handling the intrusions
coupled with the fact that nearly half of the population
seemed to be willfully and righteously ignorant, compelled
her to leave.

What kept her in Intersection Thirteen—the detail she
refused to share with Arn by way of correspondence—was
the fact that Martin was in trouble, and she felt deeply
responsible for that. She could partly justify relieving
herself of that responsibility. It had been a simple question
about a fact of the metaxia that *everyone* knew, anyone
with even the most surface understanding of the existence
of parallel worlds. But, it had been she who had spoken the
words that had sent Martin to… wherever he was now.

Mira checked her computer in vain. Still no reply from
him.

She sighed and pulled up the UMI news sources she had
come to trust. The incursions had now claimed a total of
0.4% of the total interior space of the UMI, but the rate was
higher in more populated intersections, like Intersection

Thirteen, where it was closer to 0.7%. She pondered that one over for a bit. The journalists citing the numbers expressed skepticism that population density could be a true corollary. There was no reason why metaxic incursions should be attracted to humans.

Mira checked the time. Only seven. She sent Daniel a message asking how he was doing and seeing if he wanted to chat over breakfast. Only after she sent it did she recall reading that all of Intersection Thirteen's restaurants were now closed. Unaffected kitchens had been directed to keep their kitchen staff cooking and set up a delivery service.

Twenty minutes later, she got a reply from Daniel, saying to meet her on the hangar bay floor between their ships at eight. Mira finished catching up on the news, patted and brushed down her clothes as best as she was able, then climbed down into the hangar. True to form, Daniel was already there waiting for her.

"How are you?" she asked.

He gave a weak smile. "They've gotten themselves into a real dilemma here."

She sat down facing him. "Oh?"

"Before that, there's a courier who's going to bring me breakfast. The scientists I worked with yesterday arranged it. I asked for two portions of everything, and they agreed, so we can share."

"Thank you." Mira smiled.

Daniel sat down on the floor and gestured for her to as well. As she did, the great hum of metaxic engines spinning up resonated out from somewhere behind her. At the entrance to Main Street, a group of a dozen or so people entered the hangar bay, each wearing many layers of clothes and hauling enormous suitcases on roller wheels. Soldiers directed them to a nearby ship.

After the ship beyond them dissolved into the metaxia and its engine roar faded, Daniel spoke in a very soft voice.

"It wasn't just the size of the metaxic eddy that brought this on. Their potentia generating systems were teetering on the edge when it happened."

"On the edge of what?" Mira asked.

"This," Daniel said. "Disintegration of the artificial quantum space."

"But they can stabilize areas. Certainly they'll stabilize everything in time?"

Daniel shook his head. "That's a temporary mitigation at best. I mean, it may *physically* work, but it won't *socially*. See, the whole, I don't know, let's call it the mythology of the UMI is that the potentia is this liberating force. It's taking all the potentia they've got just to stabilize half their living space. There's nothing left for anything else. No sculpting out any new spaces. No new parks. No new gardens. No new fancy architecture carved out of the metaxia."

Mira nodded. The demonstrators who wanted their 'freedom' back now made a kind of sense. It was a pathology, certainly, but now, at least, Mira could see how so many had arrived at that conclusion. They needed the comfort of the world where such power was possible, even if they only had an infinitesimal chance of wielding it.

Mira caught movement in her peripheral vision just then and turned to see a young man approaching them wearing a kitchen apron and carrying two full plastic bags. Daniel and she both stood.

"Daniel Meyer?"

Daniel stood. "That's me."

Mira stood up, too.

"Two breakfasts, sir." The courier handed out the bags and Daniel took them.

"Thank you."

"Have a good day, sir." He turned to Mira. "Ma'am."

"You, too."

Daniel handed one of the bags to her, and they both sat back down and unpacked their contents. The orange-pink meat and little peppery-tasting bits of grain were all contained within, the typical breakfast she had gotten used to from *Golden Circle*. The young man probably wasn't from *Golden Circle*, but she enjoyed the recollection of her first days in Intersection Thirteen all the same.

After they'd taken a few bites, Daniel looked over his shoulder in the direction the young man had gone. "I feel sorry for him," Daniel said.

"Oh?"

"If things get really bad, he will likely be stuck here."

It was the first time Mira had felt trepidation around Daniel. "But you're going to see if you can find a way to help, aren't you?"

"Of course," Daniel said. He sighed, put down his food, and looked squarely at her. "We know what they say about Isallna, about how 'oppressive' we are. Some very young, very immature people might gloat over this situation, but that would be juvenile. I'm not here to lord over them, tell them 'we told you so' or anything like that, much less to do anything like sabotage any hope of fixing this situation. That would make us monsters, and as Cecilia explained, people in our positions aren't allowed to be monsters. You could tell Cecilia, and Cecilia would ask for my resignation if I did such a thing."

Mira swallowed what she'd been chewing and held her plate in her lap, gripping it tightly.

"It's just," Daniel spoke very quietly now, "based on what I saw yesterday, I do not—" He seemed to almost think better of his words. "We could discover anything in the next few days, but the possibility of a solution that allows for additional potentia generation is remote at best."

"If all the Cooperatives donated their ships, could you get everyone out of the intersections? I mean, if they are at least able to stabilize spaces, that should give us enough time to get everyone out, right?"

"Possibly. I'll have my ship run the numbers on how long that would take. We should start thinking along those lines."

Mira would include that in her letter to Arn that evening. The Reconstructionists' ships couldn't hold a lot of people. She could get maybe two dozen into the Liberalis. It would be uncomfortable, but it would be something. Perhaps she would finally get to see Arn again. It was a welcome thought, even, and perhaps especially, under the circumstances.

When they'd finished eating, Mira thanked Daniel for the food.

"Let me know how it goes with the other researchers," Mira said.

"Will do." Daniel headed back towards his ship. His tone of voice betrayed a distinct lack of hope.

When Mira got back to her ship, she set herself to the task of emailing all of Martin's coworkers at *The Probability*.

She got replies back from half of them, most of them expressing a similar concern about Martin and wondering if Mira herself knew anything. She prepared a stock answer for such emails explaining that she'd been away for nearly three days and didn't know any more than they did, but she was also concerned.

A few asked for more details on metaxic organisms, and to these, Mira evaded the question completely, saying that she was just looking for Martin and she didn't have anything to share on that topic.

Around ten, she received an email from a name she recognized: Julia Kemp, the reporter Martin had introduced her to at *The Probability* offices on her visit there. The message body was brief: "Meet me in the Alesky

Gardens at 1:45 pm."

Mira accessed the map of Intersection Thirteen from *The Probability*. They were maintaining a miniature 3D representation of the entire intersection, showing which areas were being maintained, which areas had been given over to the intrusions, and which areas were slated to be given over. The map filled her whole console, and then some.

"Aurie, scale down."

The map diminished to a more manageable size. At the very edge lay the blue dot that represented her and the Liberalis in the hangar bay. A long line of connected corridors and spaces stretched out from those. Snake-like, it ran from the hangar bay all around the periphery of the intersection, forming a fat, grey U-shape. In the center of the U lay a cluster of spaces that had been tinted red. Between the two regions were a variety of orange dots. Mira glanced up at the legend, a box floating in the air above the white, orange, and red polygons. The orange areas, the legend said, were slated to be given over the incursions at 2 pm today.

"Highlight the Alesky Gardens," Mira said.

A bobbing arrow appeared atop a rectangle not too far from the hangar. It was orange, of course.

Every fiber in Mira's being willed her not to go, not to get herself further involved in this. Every instinct she had developed was screaming, "run, run, RUN." Find safety. Find shelter. Make them forget about you, make them think you have fled somewhere far away or are dead. Your life is worth more, so much more, than their ridiculous corruption. Survive for tomorrow.

Mira found herself resisting. As she had told Arn three days ago, it was time to stop running and start insisting that things be better than they were.

—

Mira left the Liberalis at 1:15 sharp and walked across the hangar bay toward the entrance to Main Street. More people with luggage on rollers were streaming toward various ships, and the sounds of metaxic engines spinning up roared through the space at regular intervals.

Mira found Main Street eerily silent. It was empty save for the individuals headed for the hangar, who all wore expressions of sadness and shock, but most of all, urgency. They rushed away, into the hangar, hauling what they could behind them. The walls were still wobbly, hazy blue, but more facades had been covered in the black haze, perhaps about a quarter of the outlines present in the walls of Main Street, which was many more than she had seen last time. Mira recalled the fat, gray U of the map just then—little specks of red and orange throughout it. Any space that had been contaminated before the fields went up, or which could be given up, had been.

As she moved further from the hangar, the foot traffic dropped to near zero. A delivery person darted quickly past her carrying bags. A lone repair person tended to an inoperative tram in the middle of the road. She didn't see a single tram in operation. She passed through Founder Square, which was also eerily empty and devoid of people, although she could see some moving furtively through the windowed walkways that connected the various structures of the space. She moved as quickly beneath them as she could without drawing attention. The guards watched her. She registered the slight turns of their heads, which set all her internal alarms. With no crowd, being seen was unavoidable. But she passed through unaccosted, and soon was out the other side of Founder Square.

Twenty minutes later, she came to the Alesky Gardens. A holographic signed posted at its entrance proclaimed its closure and the time its protective support would be relinquished.

Mira entered, and, physically, it seemed much as it had on her first visit. The trees were resplendent. The simulated sun shone, and the simulated breezes washed over her, but there were no families or students or couples, or anyone else moving about. Mira walked down the path, occasionally doubling back to check both parts of a fork. She walked the entire loop and found no one. Her computer read 1:50. Not much time.

She doubled back, deciding to do one more round.

At the very back of the gardens, she heard it—

"Mira!" It was whispered very loudly from behind a hedgerow.

Mira looked around herself—still no one—and pushed into the hedges. At first, the hedges held their ground, but as she moved to her right, she found they could be peeled away. She stepped off a path and into a grove.

Julia stood at its center, wearing some kind of track pants and trainer top. "Hello." Her expression was flat, stolid.

Mira matched her demeanor. "Hello."

"There's not much time left, so I'll get right to the point. Martin found out something about metaxic organisms. Something that disturbed him rather badly."

"He told me before I left that one of the recruiting teams ran into one. Is that it?"

Julia shook her head. "Half of the office dug into that one. That's looking like some metaxic organism messed up and contacted one of our recruiting teams, even though she wasn't supposed to. All of the recruiters who were part of that team eventually emigrated away from the UMI. All the rest of the info about it has been buried. Martin found something else, something he wasn't supposed to find."

"What was it?"

Julia's expression slumped. "You don't know?"

"No. I mean, I don't know much about metaxic organisms except that they show up when people are about to enter the metaxia for the first time. They show up and say, 'the metaxia's our home; don't mess with it.'"

Julia chortled. "We clearly never got that message."

"Or maybe you did." Mira crossed her arms.

"You mean maybe Marcus Stolten did. Such a vile man. And half the UMI practically worships him."

Mira glanced at her computer. 1:56. "How do I find Martin?"

"If the government took him, he is almost certainly somewhere in the Founder Square complex. That's the most likely scenario. But there's no way to be sure."

Mira nodded. "Thank you."

"Do you have some way of getting him out? No. Probably best if you don't tell me. I don't know anything about the technology you've got hidden away in your computer. The government's really irked that they can't hack your systems, by the way."

Mira grinned. "I've got a friend who would love to hear that, but let's not tell him. It would bloat his ego. Shall we head back?"

Julia nodded. "I'll take the left fork. You go right. After you."

Mira looked Julia over carefully. No sign of subterfuge. She decided to indeed go first, keeping a careful eye over her shoulder the whole time. Julia did not move. Mira reached the hedges and pulled them apart, then pushed through and took the right fork away from the place. She walked as quickly as she dared. As she neared the entrance, the sun dimmed, and a pale glow suffused the space. The entrance to the space took on a dark grey haze. The birds started throwing up squawks from the trees, and wings could be heard beating through the air. Mira hadn't thought until then what would happen to all the birds.

She hurried away through the dark portal, out of the now unprotected Alesky Gardens.

Mira headed back the way she had come through the empty thoroughfares. She noticed a few more facades than before had been covered in the gray haze, and she recalled that many other spaces, not just the Alesky Gardens, had been given up at the 2 pm deadline.

As she approached Founder Square, she slowed. A group of eight soldiers passed through the rectangular entrance into Founder Square from the other direction, their arms bristling with nanite-generated forcefield static. Mira slowed, crept toward the entrance, keeping a good distance between her and it, and looked inside.

Through the portal, she could see a crowd of people, perhaps fifty to a hundred of them. They stood around the cube that held the main entrance. Some held signs, and many of them were shouting. Mira could only catch a few words and phrases: "freedom," "my rights," "open up," "government," and others. All around the crowd stood the soldiers, each holding one arm up so as to cover them in a forcefield haze. The soldiers weren't advancing on the crowd or doing anything remotely threatening, but there they stood. As she watched, more soldiers entered Founder Square from its opposite entrance.

Mira grimaced and moved back, putting even more distance between her and the entrance to Founder Square. She then pulled up *The Probability*'s map on her tablet computer. She traced a path around Founder Square and back into Main Street. All of the sections were protected except for one. It was red, and it had been given over at yesterday's 2 pm deadline. That meant that it had been collecting intrusions for a full twenty-four hours. And it looked like she would have to cover a stretch about a third of a kilometer long. Did she dare?

She crept as close as she dared to the Founder Square entrance. The mob seemed to have grown louder and angrier. The soldiers were still standing motionless, but such things could change in a moment. Mira decided she would try the alternate route, and if the unprotected corridor seemed dangerous, she would come back and take her chances in Founder Square.

Mira turned and headed back the way she had come, then ducked into a side street. This street was narrower, and wooden crates had been stacked in rows. There was barely room for two people to pass each other, but the street was empty, and so she hurried past the crates. She turned next into an industrial space. Large machines whirred and hummed, and she had to weave around them. The space she came to next was filled with pipes, some opaque, some translucent, a bright blue liquid churning through them.

At the far side of that space, she pulled out her map to make sure she was still on course. After another narrow street filled with boxes and lined with greyed-out portals, she came to a greyed-out portal on the far side. She took a deep breath and stuck her head through it.

The interior was another industrial space. Large machines filled it, but these were inoperative. Mira spotted two places where the walls had bubbled out into the machines, consuming them. Two parts of the floor had bubbled up as well. The ceiling was also dotted with intrusion clusters. The lighting was very dim, but there was just enough of it to make out the outlines of the machinery.

Mira took a deep breath and entered. It was eerily silent and the clank of her footfalls reverberated about the space. She realized just then that a low background hum had been permeating the sections she'd been passing through, but not here. Not wanting to spend any more time standing on unprotected flooring than she had to, Mira hurried toward that far wall, where the map had indicated the exit would be.

With the dim light and the numerous pieces of industrial equipment in the way, she couldn't see that wall very well, and she prayed that *The Probability*'s information was accurate. She turned right around one giant piece of equipment, left around another. She approached a machine standing between her and the door.

All at once, a part of the floor just three meters in front of her bulged, noiselessly protruding upward into a sphere. Smaller spheres emerged from it and others dotted the floor.

Mira let out a small scream and scrambled back the way she'd come, weaving around a large apparatus that seemed something like a crane. She forced herself not to run, for if she ran, she would be less likely to notice a new intrusion. Her heart was pounding out of her chest, and she wanted out, out of this horrible place. She weaved around another intrusion in the floor, this one already formed and unmoving, and came to the other side of the crane apparatus.

The hazy portal out of her nightmare world came into view. Two clusters of floor intrusions lay in her path, and neither of these was visibly changing. Mira hurried forward, giving these intrusions a wide berth as well. She weaved left around the one, then right around the other. The exit was perhaps twenty meters away now, and it was a straight shot.

Mira hurried forward; she was almost there. Just as she passed through the exit, she caught a glimpse of the wall just above it, as it bulged and bubbled outward. A spike of adrenaline surged through her, and Mira dove through the gateway into the space on the other side, skidding on the floor, scrambling away as fast as she could on all fours, and gasping for breath. Mira picked herself up and observed her surroundings—normal lighting, no intrusions. She was crawling on her hands and knees in another narrow street of crates, these made of metal.

Still gasping for breath, she stood and pulled up her map. She memorized the route that would take her to Main Street and took off as fast as her feet could take her.

When Mira got back to Main Street, she put on her expression of nonchalance, although inside she was still quite shaken from her experience in the unprotected industrial room. The practiced facade proved unnecessary as Main Street now lay deserted. The tram sat, inoperative, in the center of the street, no one even attending to it. Mira didn't see anyone until she got closer to the hangar, and then it was only more emigrants, a family of six, the father carrying an infant in his arms, while mom and the older children hauled the luggage.

Mira lined up behind them to enter the hangar. She glanced at the guards with an expression of complete serenity and obliviousness, but inside she could not have been more nervous. Fortunately, she was practiced at such subterfuge.

The guards let her pass, and she hurried around a UMI ship toward the pad where the Liberalis was docked, and—

Mira stopped and had to catch her breath. The Liberalis was there, just where she'd left it, but the pad next to it, where Daniel's ship should have been, stood empty. She hurried up to the Liberalis, rushed through the airlock, and clambered into the cockpit.

"Aurie," she said, just as she was pulling open the hatch, at the same time that Aurie said, "Mira."

"Go ahead," she instructed the computer.

"You have two text transmissions waiting for you. One is from Daniel Meyer. The other is from Senator Murray."

"Load them into my computer." Mira threw down her backpack and pulled out the computer. She opened the letter from Daniel first.

Dear Mira Rous:

By the time you get this, I will be gone from the UMI. I have returned to Isallna, where I will be organizing the rest of our ships to come help with the evacuation efforts.

I had to leave quickly, because the information I have learned, and which I am about to tell you in this letter, is politically dangerous. I warn you not to share this with anyone in the UMI, but to use it to your own avail however you see fit. You strike me as the kind of person who would not take advantage of the situation, and so I am trusting you with this.

As the news has already remarked, intersections with higher population density are experiencing an increased rate of intrusion activity. This is not actually because of population density or size; rather, it is only indirectly the cause. Large populations require more potentia to generate their food and to maintain their spaces, and as I discovered today, it is potentia generation itself that is leading to the increase in intrusion activity.

The UMI's space has never been and never will be self-sustaining. Even if the metaxic eddy hadn't come along, this process would have started eventually anyway. It might have taken another hundred years, but it definitely would have happened. The eddy just kicked it into overdrive. The UMI will never generate enough potentia to permanently stabilize any of its spaces because the more potentia they generate, the stronger the pressure becomes on the existing stable spaces and the more potentia it takes to keep them stable. The only answer is to abandon the intersections entirely. All of them. This is a conclusion that many will deny. Some may even be willing to kill in order to maintain the illusion that their way of life, one fueled by potentia exploitation, is sustainable.

At the current rate of degradation, I estimate there are somewhere between twenty and thirty days remaining before the entire metaxic superstructure of the UMI collapses. A number of the researchers here have known this already for a few days, and many have suspected this would happen for years. They are men and women of science, after all. However, they are also too afraid of those in power to say or do anything except make their own preparations for departure before things get too bad.

If you wish to help, I would recommend you get your friends on Earth to bring their ships and assist with the evacuation, although I would understand if you worry that would draw the attention of your Hegemony and Equum. At the very least, you should find somewhere safe to relocate to.

I still hope that the Reconstructionists and the East Bremm Cooperative can establish a relationship on the other side of this calamity, but we will have to hold that discussion for another day.

I hope we get to meet again.

All the best,
Daniel Meyer

Mira found she had to sit down halfway through

Daniel's letter; she let herself fall into her cockpit chair, where she read through to the end. When she was finished, she took many minutes—she wasn't sure how many—to process everything she now knew. When she was ready, she pulled up Senator Murray's letter.

Call me when you receive this.

Mira almost chuckled. Almost. Worry took over too soon. She wondered what they knew of her meeting with Julia. Even if they hadn't tracked her exact movements or figured out who she'd met, they must have known that she left her ship and had learned *something* from *someone*. Or perhaps learned nothing. Make them think that, she told herself. Let them think today was a dead end in my book.

She initiated a call with Senator Murray.

"Senator Murray speaking."

"This is Mira Rous. I got your message."

"Ah, Mira. How are you doing?"

"All right, I suppose, all things considered. How about yourself?"

"Good, good. I'm confident we'll beat this thing. As you know, our scientists are working hard. Thank you again for bringing your Isallnan colleague to help us. He's contributed everything he could, and now he's gone home."

"I was wondering what had happened to his ship. I was worried about him."

"Don't worry. Nothing untoward has happened. I think this problem was out of his league, to be frank. But I do want to underscore our appreciation for your help in searching out a solution to our dilemma."

"Not a problem."

"So, what will you be doing next?"

Mira had been ready for this one. "I was wondering... I noticed a number of individuals seem to be leaving

Intersection Thirteen."

"Yes. Some of our citizens have decided to wait out this disruption to their lives on some other plane. They'll be welcome back when this is over, of course."

"Of course. That must take a lot of metaxic ships, though. My group's ships can't hold very many people, only about twenty or so each, but if it would be useful to the UMI to have six more ships at their disposal, I would be happy to extend our help."

"Yes, that offer would be welcome. Will you be heading back to Earth, then?"

"I will send my friends a message, and they will bring our other ships."

"And what will you do in the meantime?"

"I was planning on expanding the habitable space in the Liberalis. It will make my ship more useful in the relocation efforts. That work will be significantly easier if you allow me to stay in the hangar."

There was a long pause. "Yes, of course. Please keep me and Cathy Om updated on your progress."

The senator was on to her. She could tell in his voice. Mira was too good at being suspicious. It bothered her sometimes, but it was too useful a skill. It had kept her alive so far.

"Thank you, Senator. I'll let you know both about the upgrades and when I have an ETA on my friends' arrival."

"Thank you, Mira. Goodbye."

"Goodbye."

Mira spent every free moment between bread sales pondering how she could learn ruin running. In the end, she coalesced on the single opportunity that seemed even remotely viable: Enro, Hanith, Tirin, and Arn. They were the only ones she was certain were successfully running the Missoula ruins. Ergo, they were the ones she needed to learn from. But how on Earth to get them to agree?

Perhaps, she figured, they didn't have to. If she could figure out where they were staying, she could follow them out of their lodging and into the ruins. Nine months remained on her protective nanites. She decided to figure it out quickly.

One chilly, autumn evening a few months later, after learning where Tirin's group stayed through some discrete inquiries amongst trusted friends, she huddled in a ditch outside an abandoned gas station and waited. Tirin and Arn weren't present that evening, but Enro and Hanith were. They sat indoors, eating the food they'd gotten from the market earlier. Mira even saw a couple of her rolls. She couldn't hear what they were saying, so she simply sat and waited.

After what seemed like an eternity, Enro and Hanith turned out the lights, exited the gas station and, thankfully, did not get into their blue pickup truck, but headed off down the road on foot, away from the city.

Mira followed, keeping just close enough not to lose sight of them. After a few turns down progressively more abandoned side streets, they came to the fence that cordoned off the Missoula ruins. To touch the wires would mean disintegration. Here, Mira noticed, under the light of the moon, someone had fitted an iron wedge into a cut in the fence wiring, which meant that the nanites in the wires (likely to have received only rudimentary programming) would be diverted around the gap. Enro and Hanith promply crawled through it. Mira followed.

At first, the ruins didn't seem all that different from the uninhabited edges of the city. Building foundations sat deserted, giant slabs of concrete with perhaps some other stone or metal rubble lay nearby. Occasionally, a pile of the stuff loomed. After following Enro and Hanith for a few blocks though, Mira started to see buildings, some of them very large buildings, not houses. These must have been warehouses or factories or something like that. She also passed what had probably been apartment buildings, and also some very large houses. Mira had, until that point, never seen structures so large. Her mother had described to her, in a few stories, how many people in the past had lived in large homes, not just the president and his cabinet members.

Enro and Hanith went into one of the buildings Mira thought to be a warehouse, and she waited outside. She checked her computer to make sure that it was still tracking her route on its mapping software. If Enro and Hanith exited from a different side of the building, the last thing she wanted was to be stuck here.

After what seemed like an eternity of waiting, Enro and Hanith finally reappeared. They wore smiles, apparently pleased with their haul, but they had put whatever it was into a bag slung over Enro's shoulder. This irritated Mira to no end. The whole point had been to discover what it was they were hauling out of here.

All at once, Mira realized that the two men were heading towards her.

"Show yourself, now!" Enro roared.

Mira gulped and shot through with fear. Her instincts drove her to crouch down as far she could and conceal herself to the maximum extent possible.

Enro and Hanith grew closer.

"We know you're there." Hanith's voice.

Perhaps this was her chance, Mira decided. Fighting every instinct, she stood up slowly, hands held high.

"I warn you not to touch me," Mira said. "I'm running protectors."

"Well, shit," Hanith said. They'd both come within a few meters of her. "The baker lady? You're kidding, right?"

"Your cover fooled us. Now, how much to not get us

reported? Out with it!"

"How much...?"

Rage flared in Enro's eyes. "Don't play with me! How much? Now. We aren't sticking around here any longer than we have to."

"I—" Mira gathered her confidence, stood up straight as she could. "I wanted to learn ruin running."

Hanith blinked. Enro smirked.

Mira crossed her arms. They would, at the very least, take her seriously.

"You're not joking," Enro said.

"No," Mira replied.

"Don't you want that nice little stall of yours to keep on going? Don't you want to live a nice quiet life? If you have any desire to continue that—"

"No," Mira stated, thinking of everything her parents had taught her, how much they'd invested in her, and how they'd been rewarded for it. She thought of Pelna and her son Rei, too. "I don't."

Enro and Hanith looked at one another. Enro twisted up his lips and widened his eyes. Hanith shrugged. Enro pulled open the bag, pulled out a book, a thick one, and handed it to Mira.

"*The Michelangelo Tapestry* by Robert Grey," Mira read from the cover. She cracked it open and skimmed the pages. Words and words and words, flowing in one enormous, unbroken block of text down the page. No lists, no instructions, no pictures, just one gushing flow of words.

"It's probably not any good," Enro said.

"Most of them aren't," Hanith admitted. "But every so often we strike gold."

"Gold?" Mira looked up. "What kind of gold?"

Enro grinned. "Literature."

-23

Dear Arn,

The UMI is in serious trouble. The researcher who came with me from Isallna has gone back. He is gathering up the metaxic ships there to help ferry people away. This isn't widely known yet but, according to that scientist, the UMI has twenty to thirty days before their entire metaxic superstructure collapses, and I know for a fact that they can't move their entire population in that time.

When the others get back from their missions, empty out their ships' cabins of everything except food and water and send them here. I'm sending coordinates with this message.

I hope you've been well these few weeks. It will be good to see you again. I hope that's soon.

Love,
Mira

Mira had meal rations for breakfast that morning. She sat in the Liberalis cockpit and reviewed the news. *The Probability* had updated its map with information from the government as to which spaces were to be sacrificed to the intrusions today. There were more orange spots than there had been the day before. Also, a bulge had formed in the right interior side of the U, a cluster of protected spaces that needed to stay protected since they surrounded the Gyrospire. Most of the spaces around Founder Square remained untouched as well. But away from that central hub, the reductions were dramatic.

Mira found other reports in the news. Particularly in other intersections, citizens were refusing to stay out of unprotected areas. They were attempting to go about their jobs and earn potentia, even as employers became unable to pay them, even as equipment failed because chunks of it were being eaten up by intrusions, and even as workers themselves lost feet and hands to sudden eruptions from the floors and walls. There had even been more than a hundred intrusion-related deaths, and the number was increasing by the hour. This portion of the population remained insistent that there was, in fact, no problem, and that their government was conspiring to deny them pay.

She found herself growing angry when she read such accounts. Mira wished that the Hegemony government had bothered to protect *its* citizens in the way that UMI was doing. They might be in denial about their ultimate vulnerability, but at least they were marking out safe and unsafe areas. They even allowed those citizens to protest the very restrictions that kept them safe! If the Hegemony were running the show, anyone the leaders didn't like would have been locked into an unprotected area and left to fend for themselves.

'Oppression.' What a bunch of garbage. These people didn't know what oppression was.

And then, she reminded herself, no matter what any of them did, a large percentage of the population, within a month, were going to die utterly senseless deaths. And it wasn't fair to them. Not by far.

Mira put away the news and refocused her thoughts on her plan for the day. One problem at a time, she decided. The plan she had devised would be incredibly risky. The UMI possessed nanotechnology as well, so there was no telling what they would and would not be able to detect. If she were found out, it could be very, very bad for her. She reminded herself of her new mantra: no more running. She would act, and to the best of her ability, she would act properly. She would behave towards her fellow human beings with compassion when it was justified, and she would be stern and harsh with them too, when it was justified. She would be fair.

She possessed the power. Was she up to the task of using it well? Could the UMI counter her? She decided she would counter first.

At ten in the morning, Mira had gathered together everything she would need. She stripped down to a pair of shorts and a light t-shirt. She would not wear her backpack for fear of the noise it would make. She would carry her computer, and thus the nanite controls, in her hand.

Mira took a deep breath and decided that she was ready to do this.

She activated the nanite program that caused them to refract light around her form, rendering her essentially invisible. She climbed out the airlock and down onto the deck making as little noise as possible. She stepped carefully onto the hangar floor and gazed around herself. Fortunately, the only other people around were refugees, all of them too focused on getting into their ships to pay attention to any noises coming from the Liberalis. The guards, too, were focused on the departing citizens.

So far so good.

Mira walked, as quietly as she could across the hangar bay towards the entrance. When she got near it, she slid around a couple talking to one of the guards at the door and tip-toed onto Main Street until she was far enough away from the door. She then proceeded at a normal pace down the deserted street toward Founder Square.

The tram still sat, abandoned, where it had been the day before. Up and down Main Street, more facades contained notices that their interiors would become unsafe at 2 pm and any residents within were to evacuate immediately. Where the evacuated tenants were supposed to go live remained unclear. Mira had read reports earlier in the morning from the poorer intersections that homelessness was on the rise and that not everyone had been able to acquire even temporary housing.

Mira drew closer to the entrance to Founder Square. Now would come the real test. This would be the highest security area in the UMI. Would her nanites fool even the detection systems here? Mira crept through the passageway into Founder Square as silently as she could, not noticing even so much as a blink from the guards standing on either side of the archway. She continued to move as quietly as she could toward the blue cube at the center of the room.

She drew closer to them. Closer still.

No movement.

She moved as carefully as she possibly could through the open passage into the cubic building. A reception desk lay in front of her, and rows of chairs to her left and right. Hallways led away from the desk, one to the left and one to the right, each containing a pair of guards. A clerk sat at the desk, reading a tablet computer and looking bored. Mira guessed that the chairs were for citizens to wait their turn at being helped, but with the emergency ongoing, most of those administrative operations, whatever they were, must have been shut down.

She decided to take the right hallway and snuck carefully down it, watching the guards carefully. She came to a T-intersection and turned left. At another juncture, she turned right. The doors in the hallways were labeled, but she found none that seemed to be a jail or a confinement area. "Immigration," "Social Services Bureau," "Labor and Statistics," "Agriculture," "Construction Permits," "Economic Development." They went on and on.

Mira crossed a walkway into another cube and found more hallways and more doors. Then she found her way to a third cube.

After two hours of walking, her stomach started to rumble, and she grew concerned that it would be audible. She was also growing weary of the tedium of the cubes' interiors, the labyrinthine hallways, the beige carpeting, and the omnipresent soft light.

At around one in the afternoon, her legs getting tired and her stomach unhappier than ever, she came to the fourth cube, and here it was that she started seeing more promising doors. "Security," "Justice"— Aha! "Corrections and Detainment."

She stopped by that door. She looked down the hallway to the left, then to the right. She waited, holding her breath, while a woman in a business suit walked past her, then disappeared around a corner. Mira pulled the door slowly open and peeked inside. No one was near.

She held her computer, now invisible, near her face.

"Decrypt locking mechanism. In front of me. Half a meter." Zekk had programmed the verbal interface for when they were invisible and couldn't see the computer's screen. He'd said it was a piece of cake. Mira and Arn had rolled their eyes at his display of ego, but they had remained eternally grateful as the program had gone on to save Reconstructionists' lives on multiple occasions.

She crept inside and pulled the door carefully shut.

A long hallway presented itself with rows of cells on each side, and no guards here. Plenty of them had been wandering about the hallways. If they figured there was no need to post more here, then the hallway was being surveilled somewhere.

"Search for surveillance and fix video to last thirty seconds, repeated," she told her computer. She wouldn't tell Zekk that this one had come in handy again. Not right away, anyway.

After her computer vibrated helpfully to inform her that the video surveillance had indeed been fixed, Mira proceeded to check through the window in the door of each cell. Halfway down the hallway, and after more than a good number of empty cells, Mira wondered if Martin were even here at all. At last, she came to the seventh from the last cell in the hallway and found him hunkered inside on the floor, hands wrapped around his head. Now was the time to pray very hard that Zekk's unlocking program had worked. Mira ordered the cell door decrypted and slipped inside.

Martin shot to a stance. "Who's there?"

"Shh!" Mira whispered. "Keep your voice down. Just in case."

Martin blinked. "Mira? You're… invisible?"

"Nanites bending light around me. Yes. Now stay completely still so I can do the same to you."

"There's something you have to know."

"You can tell me back at the Liberalis."

"No, there's something else we have to do here."

"It will have to wait. This is dangerous enough."

"No, Mira. Listen. We have to do this now. They have a metaxic organism. Here in Intersection Thirteen. In Founder Square. They're holding him hostage. That's why the rest of the metaxic organisms don't come near us, why they haven't torn the UMI apart. Our leaders have been threatening to kill him if they do."

It took every last bit of mental willpower Mira possessed to restrain herself from shouting. A metaxic organism? *Hostage*? Of all the completely unethical, *utterly stupid* things a society could do, this had to be at the top of the list. She could not have made that one up. Not in a million years. Such thoughts hurtled through her mind in the space of milliseconds, her emotions ablaze. Then, she reminded herself, there were the cameras. It was only a matter of time before someone noticed a discrepancy, and then high alert mode would be engaged.

"Martin," she said, calmly and quietly. "I've tampered with the monitoring equipment, but that won't last forever. If we are still here, in Founder Square, when high alert mode is activated, we will both be in serious trouble."

"We have to try to free him."

"I can't believe—" He was going to insist they do the right thing. Right action. She had told Arn she was going to stop running. She was going to take a stand for what she believed in. Well, that's what she got for reading all that Plato and Aristotle and Marcus Aurelius.

Mira sighed a sharp sigh. "All right. Do you know where he is?"

"Not exactly, but I learned that the technology to restrain him eats a ton of potentia. Can your computer find power sources?"

"It could if I could see it."

"You said you tampered with the cameras."

He had a point. She held the computer close. "Unveil all."

Martin chuckled.

"I didn't make that up," she insisted. "One of my colleagues did." And she promptly proceeded to search out power sources in Founder Square. Within a minute, the results came back. In one of the previous cubes she'd been in, there was a powerful energy field, the quanta practically streaming off it.

Mira showed Martin the map. "We won't be able to consult the map once we leave. Can you memorize the path there?"

Martin nodded.

"We're about to both be invisible. I will take the right side of a hallway. You take the left. If we come to an intersection, we stop, we wait for any passersby, and then we both snap our fingers, once for straight ahead, twice for left, and three time for right. Then we proceed. Same if someone passes us in the hallway. Stop and snap when they're gone. That way we don't lose each other. If we do get separated, go back to the Liberalis and wait for me at the ladder. Make sense?"

Martin nodded again.

Mira held the computer close. "Veil Martin."

Martin shimmered out of sight.

"Veil all," Mira commanded, and she and her computer shimmered to invisibility as well.

Mira snapped. Martin snapped in response.

Mira opened the cell door and exited. She snapped again. Martin's responded. She shut the door and walked down the right side of the hallway to the very end. She snapped. A delay. Was he already lost? Moments later, she heard Martin's snap.

They proceeded through the monotonous Founder Square hallways in the same fashion, stopping for intersections, for people, snapping when it was safe to proceed. They walked for nearly twenty minutes. More than once, Mira grew afraid that Martin had forgotten the way or that someone had heard them snap. A new person would show up after another had left down a hallway and they would have to wait all over again. Founder Square was getting busier.

They crossed the translucent walkway into their target cube building and wound through numerous hallways, moving much more slowly than Mira would have liked. Any minute now, a UMI official would figure out that the video of the cells was on repeat, she thought. And that got her thinking about the metaxic organism *hostage* and just how ridiculously stupid that had been. Probably Marcus Stolten's doing. The more she learned about him, the more she disliked him. And here were all these people, living in an artificial universe falling apart around them because an idiot like Stolten needed to achieve conquest and glory. Humanity in any universe should have seen his form of "glory" enough times to know that it has never ended well for the conquerors. The fall of Athens, the fall of Rome, the fall of Constantinople, the fall of... whatever there had been in the twenty-first century, that haze of literature that ended with a handful of writers. Such a tragedy and a waste.

The two of them came to their target door. A large symbol lay plastered on it that Mira didn't recognize, and she didn't like it. It had jagged, pointy edges, and its shape reminded her of a parallel earth macropathogen she had once encountered.

Mira snapped, and Martin responded.

She ordered her computer to hack the door, the same as she had done to enter Martin's cell. She hoped this was truly where they were holding a metaxic organism and not the biological warfare division. That would not end well for them, though there was no way to be sure that meeting a captive metaxic organism would go any better. Mira had never heard of one harming humans on any world, but then she had never heard of them being imprisoned by humans for nearly three centuries, either.

As Mira and Martin crept inside, a blue glow washed over them, making their forms momentarily visible. But the effect faded, and they were invisible again. Mira shut the door.

"Mira and Martin." The strange voice was accompanied by a small laugh. "Welcome."

Mira jumped and spun around. The room was spacious. Desks, chairs, computer equipment, and cabinets all lined the walls. No people were present, but at the center of the room was a box of blue energy perhaps ten meters square. Within lay a bed, a chair, and a desk. Sitting at the chair, facing toward the door, sat a man. He was tall, and he might have been handsome except for the strange effect upon his skin. Bubbles of blue pushed upwards against his skin from the inside, then retreated. They burst out all across his body, making his visage somewhat hideous.

"Finally," the man said. "It's almost over."

"Are you… a metaxic organism?" Martin asked.

The man nodded.

"I am so, *so* sorry for what's been done to you," Martin said. "If I had *ever* known, I would have torn this whole place apart myself."

The man nodded, his expression sad. "You and many other citizens of the UMI."

"What is your name?" Mira asked.

"Kalos," the man said.

"How can we release you?" Martin asked.

Kalos sat quietly for many moments, then shook his

head slowly from side to side. "You needn't."

"*I* need to," Martin said. "This is wrong. Utterly wrong."

"Martin." The metaxic organism pulled himself up, seeming to expend a great amount of energy doing so. He took a step forward, clasped his hands behind his back, and looked directly at the place where Martin stood, despite the fact that Mira's nanites had rendered him invisible. "In another twelve days, the potentia supply to Founder Square will fail. The technology that restricts me to this cube will deactivate, and I will be free once more to do as I please."

"There's nothing I can do? I can't release you?" Martin's voice sounded weak. "Nothing I can do to make this right?"

Kalos gave him a smile, the saddest smile Mira had ever seen. "No."

Mira reached out for Martin's arm but couldn't find it. "Let's go, Martin."

"No!" Martin roared. "I won't let this continue!"

"Martin." Mira's sense of danger flared. "What are you doing?"

Cabinet doors on the far side of the room began flying open, then the frenetic activity moved to the desk. Computers flew up from their places and crashed against the wall.

"Unveil all," Mira ordered her computer.

She ran to Martin as he picked up another computer and hurled it into the wall. She grabbed his arms and tried to restrain him, but he broke free from her grasp and went after another computer.

"Martin! Stop!"

"I'm setting him free."

"You can't, Martin! You can't." She grabbed his arm as he reached out for yet another computer and held it with all her strength. "You can't fix this. It's been wrong for a very long time. It was never right from the start, and now, even if you free him, the UMI is still done. It can't sustain itself. The researchers all know it. Potentia generation creates the intrusions. Potentia will never produce enough of itself to be sustainable. If Kalos knows that he will escape, let him escape that way. They perceive time differently from us. Twelve days to him is nothing."

She threw down his arm.

Martin turned slowly to Kalos. "Is that true?"

"Yes," Kalos said. "My three centuries here in your time is nothing to me. It is similar in scope to the detainment you have just experienced, a little over two days. Hardly anything at all in the grand scheme of my life. And I have hardly been mistreated."

"You knew they would never follow through on their threat, didn't you?" Mira asked.

Kalos gave them a wry smile and sat down.

He turned his head slightly. "You should both go now. They will be here soon. If you don't go now, you won't escape."

"Veil all," Mira told her computer, and she and Martin disappeared.

She moved to the door and snapped. Martin was silent. Was he fit for travel? Would she have to leave him? She hoped she wouldn't have to do that.

Martin snapped, finally, and Mira opened the door.

As she left, she looked over her shoulder to Kalos. He wore a bemused expression, both content and serene. It was as though, after some not terribly brief but also not too wearisome period of time, he would be able to go home. At least, that was what she imagined. Who knew what kind of thoughts pervaded the minds of metaxic organisms?

Mira didn't have any trouble getting Martin out of Founder Square. When they reached the lobby, just as they were walking to the exit, a group of guards charged from the left hallway down the right, the way they had just come. Even the bored clerk at the desk had jumped to attention. Mira tiptoed carefully out the door, across the plaza, and once she reached a safe distance from the Main Street guards, she snapped.

At first, nothing. She waited a few moments and snapped again.

Martin responded that time.

They proceeded down Main Street in that manner, Mira snapping every so often and Martin snapping in reply. She didn't even break stride to do so, since the street was completely deserted. A few food couriers passed, but that was all.

They reached the door to the hangar, and proceeded to the ladder of the Liberalis. Once they were both inside the airlock, Mira deactivated the invisibility nanites and looked Martin over.

"What?" Martin asked defensively.

"How are you doing?"

"What kind of question is that?"

That was somewhat more than Mira could take. "I did just risk my life to break you out of jail. You're welcome." She clambered up the ladder. Unbelievable.

Martin followed her.

"Close the hatch," she said.

Martin closed it, then turned to her. "Thank you. I really do appreciate it. Though please recall that I just learned that my entire civilization is about to collapse. And that it's founded on injustice." He squatted down and wrapped his arms around his head.

Mira deflated. "Come here."

She guided him to the cockpit chair and let him sit down.

He shook his head. "I'm a complete fool."

"You're not."

"No, really. My whole life I thought that if I could give people enough information, if I could just write about life well enough, I could make people see how lucky we all were, how—with a little hard work, with a little effort—it could all hold together. But it's all been a lie. Everything."

Mira sat down from him. "So, the UMI lied to you." She wondered momentarily if she should hold back and promptly decided not to. "I'm sorry, but big deal. I'm certain most everything I've been taught by my government is lies."

Martin shook his head. "Can I really live with such a thing?"

"Yes."

He turned and looked at her with such intense longing. "How?"

Mira smiled, just a little. "Well, the story starts with this man named Plato. He and his teacher lived in a society that was full of lies, too, but his teacher was the only one who could see them. He taught Plato how to think critically about his world, how to imagine a better one. Most of the citizens of Athens didn't respond to the teacher like Plato did, though. They saw him as an annoyance. They had practical concerns to get on with. No time to think about whether things were good or bad. The whole city turned against Plato's teacher, and eventually they succeeded in prosecuting him on false charges and had him killed. We know Plato was devastated because he wrote stories about his teacher's trial, his imprisonment, and his death—all at the hands of the very people whose lives that man was trying to make better by teaching them how to really *think*. Plato was so angry at what happened that he wrote stories. He enshrined his teacher's vision of the world in dramatic narratives, and for almost three millennia now, we've read his words. When we do, we realize that no matter how awful our leaders are, no matter how oppressive our society gets, no matter how many stupid people destroy however many beautiful things, we can still have our dignity. It's because our freedom, real freedom, doesn't come from treasures or money or power or legitimacy or recognition or anything else outside of us. Freedom comes from inside." Mira smirked. "And from a million minor acts of defiance. Like standing up for what you believe in. Like trashing a government laboratory because you can't stand the injustice it represents. I was proud of you just then, you know. I wanted to kick your ass, sure, but I was also proud of you."

Martin deflated, smiled, and leaned in. Mira put a hand up to her mouth instinctively and stood. "And, sorry, but another thing you should finally know about me is that I'm with someone. On Earth. I appreciate how you taught me about the UMI and showed me around and were honest with me about everything, but that's as far as it goes. All right?"

Martin nodded morosely. "What do we do now?"

"For the time being, we wait."

Martin stared blankly into the large computer wall monitor.

Mira sighed, sat herself in the back of the cockpit by the lockers, and got to work on her computer. She could free up *some* space in the Liberalis. She hadn't been completely lying to the senator, after all.

Mira begged Enro and Hanith to let her take the copy of *The Michelangelo Tapestry* they'd found, but they refused. Instead, they took her with them into the next building and told her how to prepare a proper hiding place for books in her house. The Hegemony had drones, which Mira had seen flying through the sky and scampering across the ground every so often, but she had never thought too much about them.

"Those drones spew out nanites," Hanith explained.

"And those nanites search out books. They know the configuration of every approved book—all your cookbooks, all your manuals, all your diagrams, every last one of them. If they find anything else, they'll scan its interior and upload it to the Hegemony database. To store fiction at home, you need a proper safe. And when you're reading, you need to be close enough to the safe to hide the book if your computer detects a drone."

Mira must have looked forlorn because Enro quickly jumped in. "Don't worry. I'm sure almost anything we find is bound to be better than *The Michelangelo Tapestry*."

"What makes you say that?" Hanith asked.

"We found another Robert Grey book once. I didn't make it past page fifty."

They scoured two more buildings that night but came up with naught.

After they'd climbed back through the wedge in the fence, Mira asked to join them on their next run. They looked at each other, and then Enro said, "meet us right here tomorrow night at eleven."

She found out later that Hanith had almost vetoed the entire proposition, but Enro's logic had won out: "She's the village *baker*, for crying out loud. I'm sorry, but that's *way* too sophisticated a ploy for the Hegemony. She's got to be legit."

Mira ran with them for the next two weeks, until they packed their haul into their pickup truck and drove back to Spokane. They returned four times over the following five months and Mira ran with them each time. By then, she'd constructed a nanite-proof safe and had read about a dozen of the books she'd found on her runs with Enro and Hanith. The first one that struck her as particularly good was *Catcher in the Rye* by J. D. Salinger. She also discovered a fondness for C. S. Lewis's *The Lion, the Witch, and the Wardrobe*, and was startled to learn from Hanith, who particularly liked fantastic fiction, that her book was only one in a whole series of Narnia books.

"Why does the Hegemony bother destroying this stuff?" Mira had asked during one of their runs.

"Control," Enro had answered. "Think about the difference between advertisements and these books. When you watch or read an advertisement, it's making you think you're not pretty enough, or not smart enough, or not something enough, and then it's providing you a way to spend money to get that thing easily. It stops you from thinking. It encourages you to solve all your problems the quick way. But literature isn't like that. Literature shows you how complex and messy human life is. It helps you realize that you're part of something bigger than yourself. When you read literature, if you pay attention, you'll realize you can't go through life completely dependent on this big, evil monstrosity because it will never make you truly happy. That's why they're afraid of it."

Mira had gone right on reading. And when she felt confident, she started doing her own runs into the Missoula ruins. When her nanites were about to expire, she bought a year's extension, even though it cost half her savings, but it was worth it to get more books. When she finished books, she handed them over to Enro and Hanith to take back to Spokane, where they said they had bigger safes. She would find out later that what they had was, in fact, a large, shielded library, fully protected from the drones, and where an even more ambitious project was beginning.

Two years after she first followed Enro and Hanith into the ruins, Mira "struck gold."

In the ruins of a hotel, she found three tomes stashed in a bedside drawer: Mary Shelley's *Frankenstein*, H. G. Well's *The War of the Worlds*, and Aldous Huxley's *Brave New World*. She ran home immediately that night and read *Frankenstein*, enthralled. She was so enraptured that she skipped running her stall that day so that she could also read *The War of the Worlds* and *Brave New World*.

A month later, Enro and Hanith showed up, and the trio met at eleven by the wedge in the fence, just as usual. However, instead of diving inside the ruins, Mira stood in front of it. "You're doing something with literature in Spokane, aren't you?"

Enro and Hanith looked at one another.

"I want in. Whatever it is. If it's with literature, I want in on it. I'll give up the stall and the house. Just let me come with you. I'll do anything you need me to do to help. Well, almost anything, if you know what I mean."

Enro held up a calming hand. "We got it. We're definitely not into anything like that."

"Well?" Hanith raised an eyebrow at Enro.

Enro shrugged. "We'll check with Tirin and let you know next month, all right? No promises, but be ready to pack up and go if it's a yes. And be ready to let us know if you still want to go running with us if it's a no."

Mira nodded and said nothing more when they ran that night.

Enro, Hanith, and Tirin all came to visit her just three weeks later. Tirin only had to speak with her briefly. It was a yes. She left on the spot. She gave the deed to her house to her favorite neighbors. She let the bread stall lease lapse.

The only things she took with her were the clothes on her back, a few dozen rolls of bread, and her small, homemade safe, the one filled with her precious books.

−21

Dear Arn,

Sorry I missed sending a letter yesterday. I got yours. I should be back at Intersection Thirteen in time to meet you when you and the others arrive. Yesterday evening I went back to Isallna. I have a lot to catch you up on.

I broke a journalist out of jail in Intersection Thirteen yesterday. I felt guilty because it was indirectly my fault he was there. He started digging for information on metaxic organisms because I had asked him about them. The UMI has been burying information about them because they've been holding one hostage. I wish I could see your face as you read this. No, I'm not joking. The UMI found a way to contain a metaxic organism somehow, and they've been *threatening to kill him if the metaxic organisms move against the UMI. I even met the organism. His name is Kalos. He didn't seem too worried about his predicament. In fact, he told us to just leave him there, saying he would be able to escape soon on his own.*

I couldn't leave the journalist anywhere in the UMI, so I took him to Isallna yesterday evening. I took the opportunity to meet up with my contacts in East Bremm. They've been working with the other cooperatives to organize an evacuation effort for the intersections. It turns out that the whole place is completely unstable. Their method of harvesting potentia from metaxic contortions is what causes their space to degrade. It will never be self-sustaining because the more they harvest, the worse the problem gets and the more potentia they need in order to stabilize their spaces—a feedback loop. Most cooperatives on Isallna are agreeing to take up to 2,000 UMI citizens, but that's only a fraction of their population. East Bremm and a few other cooperatives are surveying worlds, trying to find one that the UMI refugees can safely evacuate to.

I'm leaving Isallna with the evacuation fleet in a couple of hours. It will be good to see you again, even under the circumstances. Take care!

Love,
Mira

Mira sat on board the Liberalis, flying it toward Intersection Thirteen and listening to Aurie recite *Behemoth*. The bridge clock showed ten in the morning. She and the rest of the Isallnan fleet would arrive in about an hour, which would be just before Arn's noon arrival. She wanted to enjoy as much of the book as possible now, because the work of getting people off Intersection Thirteen was likely to be difficult, perhaps even dangerous. Arn had agreed with her though—they had an ethical obligation to save as many lives as possible. They couldn't just stand by and let more than 600 million people be metaxically crunched out of existence.

Aurie ceased reciting *Behemoth*. "There is an incoming transmission. It's Daniel Meyer."

"Put him through."

"Mira?"

"Hi, Daniel. Everything all right?"

"Everything's fine with the fleet. Is your equipment able to pick up UMI public broadcasts from here?"

"It should be. Why?"

"Intersection Thirteen has canceled their evacuation and is recalling their evacuated citizens. They're saying they've fully stabilized their livable space and halted the advance of the incursions. And something else. Intersections 5, 17, and 42 are gone."

"Gone?" Mira shot to a stance. "What is gone?"

"Founder Square is saying that they have experienced total structural collapse owing to their local government's mismanagement. Those spaces have been fully intruded."

"Does everyone believe that? No one thinks it suspicious that these two events are co-occurring rather conveniently?"

"You and I both know the real cause of the intrusions, but the people of the UMI mostly still think that it's a problem caused by the metaxic eddy and they only need to wait for science to find a way to stabilize a metaxic contortion. Intersection Thirteen is saying they've done just that."

Mira rubbed her hands over her face. "How would causing another intersection's destruction help Intersection Thirteen stabilize itself, anyway?"

195

"I don't know. Anyway, we're still an hour out, so we've got some time to think this through. I'll keep myself tuned into their media, and I suggest you do the same."

"Thanks, Daniel."

Mira requested that Aurie save her place in *Behemoth* and begin searching through the Intersection Thirteen media. After a momentary pause, he responded with headline titles declaring safety and stability in Intersection Thirteen. No new spaces were scheduled to be given over to the intrusions today, and some workplaces were being reopened and their intrusions sculpted away. The government had announced a phased approach to bringing businesses and services back online.

Another article contained the information that Daniel had mentioned, about how Intersections 5, 17, and 42 had experienced a sudden and dramatic increase in intrusion activity. One by one, the stabilization barriers had failed, and within minutes, the intrusions had obliterated those intersections' entire interior. She had Aurie read that article to her in full. The most interesting element to Mira—presented as a kind of aside or afterthought in the articles—was the indication that Founder Square might send out scientists to other intersections to assess the coherence of their integrity systems, along with bureaucrats to evaluate whether those systems were being managed properly.

Mira ordered Aurie to stop his recitation. She felt sick to her stomach. Everything she'd done, everything she'd gone through. So much for the failure of Intersection Thirteen within twelve days. It looked like Kalos wasn't on track to escape after all. Mira tapped her fingers on the console. Forty minutes left. Nothing to do but wait.

She asked Aurie to continue reading *Behemoth* to her, just where they'd left off.

—

Once they'd arrived at Intersection Thirteen, Mira parked the Liberalis in the metaxia and ordered Aurie to cease his recitation. She then began tracking the progress of Arn and the four other Reconstructionist ships alongside him. Their dots slid arduously across her monitor. Then, finally, a shimmer in the blue to her left became tiny dots of ships, slowly growing larger, then larger still.

A video box appeared on her monitor screen and Mira's heart leapt.

"This is Captain Arn Hosh of the Reconstructionists. We've arrived in response to a request for humanitarian aid."

Mira couldn't help but smile seeing Arn's face appear on the screen. He hadn't shaved in about a week, and his hair was a mess, which tended to happen while Mira was away, but in that moment she hardly cared. That was the Arn she loved.

"Hello, Captain Hosh." Cathy appeared on the other half of her monitor. Mira's smile fell. "Thank you for responding to our request. Professor Meyer, are you still connected?"

Daniel appeared in a third rectangle upon her screen. "I am."

Cathy continued. "Captain Hosh, this is Professor Daniel Meyer, organizer of the Isallnan fleet."

"A pleasure," Arn said.

"Likewise," Daniel said.

Cathy smiled serenely. "Well then. Let me get you all up to speed. Intersection Thirteen is now stable, but we have a number of Intersections we are now concerned about, particularly Intersections 1, 20, 26, and 34. Please focus your evacuation efforts there."

"Cathy." Arn furrowed his brow. "I'm told that some intersections have suddenly and rapidly collapsed. Is that correct?"

"It is."

"How will we know if that is happening again?"

"It is unlikely, but we will broadcast emergency alerts on all frequencies if another intersection begins experiencing such a failure."

"Thank you. I'm happy to help, but I also need to look out for the safety of my crew."

"It's understandable. We would do the same for our own citizens. Thank you again for your assistance."

"We're happy to help."

After the group video cut out, Mira initiated a direct call to Arn. He smiled at her over the camera, shook his head, and made a tsk tsk sound. "What have you gotten yourself into out here, Mira?"

"What have you done to your face?"

"I like my beard, thank you."

"Try kissing someone with a beard sometime."

"Enro says it's not that bad."

Mira rolled her eyes. "He would. Thanks for coming."

Arn waved his hands out. "Humanitarian aid. It's a no-brainer. If we ignored stuff like this, it would make us no better than the Hegemony or the Equum."

"Let's get on with this then. The sooner we start, the sooner I can see you again in person."

"Roger that."

Mira ended the call and began to set the Liberalis helm for a path to Intersection Twenty. Before she could initiate the engines, she got a call notification from Daniel.

"Daniel?"

"Hello, Mira."

"What is it?"

"The transmission is encrypted on your end, too, right?"

Mira tapped at her computer console. "I am now."

"Something's not right."

"What? A trap?"

"Not at the intersections Cathy listed, no. I've found *something*. I'm not certain, but I think that Intersection Five's hangar is still intact and stable. And I think that other spaces might be stable, too."

"Could the intersection still be there somehow?"

"I'm not sure. I'm going to go investigate it."

"Let Arn and me do it."

"All three of us will go."

Mira thought that over. It was a far better idea than any one of them going alone. "Send me the coordinates. I'll talk to Arn. We should all try to set down in the hangar at the same time."

Daniel ended the call with an anxious nod. Mira relayed the new plan to Arn, and within minutes they were underway, not toward Intersection Twenty but whatever was left of Intersection Five.

The blue whorls of the metaxia dissipated, and darkness formed in its place. It was very dark, almost pitch black.

"Aurie," Mira ordered, "external lights."

Mira could now see a floor, that same hazy, wobbly blue floor that comprised the interior of Intersection Thirteen. And there was definitely a ring on the floor, indicating a landing pad. She could also see the shape of Arn's ship on her right, and Daniel's ship on her left. In the distance, some red and green lights flickered in the outline of a door.

Mira reached for the communication controls, intending to connect Daniel and Arn into a single call, but she was interrupted.

"Proximity alert," Aurie said.

"What is it?"

"People," Aurie replied. "Two are approaching the ship."

"Show me."

The monitor switched to an aft view. Two young men

approached, their faces covered in grime, or perhaps it was dried blood. One of them was shirtless, and his left arm was either covered in a mass of black or he didn't have a left arm at all. It was hard to tell. In his right hand, he held a pipe with a jagged end of torn-up metal. The other man carried a blade with a jagged edge. The two of them lashed out at the Liberalis with their weapons, and Mira heard clangs from below.

"Structural damage," Aurie said.

"Execute soporos!" Mira roared. She watched the forms of the men. They hit the ship's landing gear a few more times, and the ship lurched. The bridge shuddered, tilting backward. Then, the two men wobbled on their feet and fell, crashing to the floor.

Mira inhaled and exhaled deeply.

"Can the damage be repaired?" she asked.

"Yes," Aurie replied.

"How long?"

"Ninety-one minutes and thirty-two seconds."

"Initiate repairs."

"Your ally's ship is under attack," Aurie said.

Mira grimaced. "Show me."

The camera switched to a view of Daniel's ship. Three men were attacking it with similarly crude weaponry.

"Run soporos on anyone in this hangar now and anyone who enters it besides me, Arn, and Daniel."

Mira opened the communication channel.

"I saw that," Arn said. "How are you both doing?"

"I'll be repaired in an hour and a half."

"I do not think I will take off again without significant repairs," Daniel said. "My metaxic engines are down. What happened to our attackers just now?"

"It's a program our colleague Zekk wrote," Mira said. "It puts people to sleep. How's your ship, Arn?"

"I'm fine. What happened here?"

"That is a very good question," Daniel said. "I started mapping the interior the moment we arrived. I'm transmitting to you now."

A 3D map appeared before Mira. It was a single chain of connected space, starting in the hangar bay and terminating in a very tall room about a kilometer away.

"That last room," Mira said. "Is that the gyrospire for Intersection Five?"

"Gyrospire?" Arn asked.

"It's the potentia generator for the intersection," Mira explained.

"And I show it as active," Daniel said.

"Active..?" All at once, it clicked into place. The single path preserved from the hangar to the spire. Just in case someone needed to show up and make repairs. Mira gulped. "It's not just powering the remaining rooms here, is it?"

"My guess is that it is not," Daniel said.

"Intersection Thirteen?" Arn tried.

"That would explain why they didn't have to give up any rooms today."

"But then, that would mean that they killed a bunch of people in order to stabilize their own space." Arn's expression turned malevolent.

"About twenty million people," Daniel said. "If my census information isn't too badly out of date."

Arn shook his head. "What kind of people would do that?"

"The same kind of people who would hold a metaxic organism hostage," Mira replied.

Arn screwed up his face.

"We should not be involved in this any further," Daniel said. "Cecilia would never condone it. Nor would the other Cooperatives, I'm sure."

"I agree," Mira said. "Arn?"

"I'm convinced," Arn mumbled through his scowl.

"How about this," Mira suggested. "Daniel, you go over to Arn's ship. Get a full complement of Intersection Twenty refugees and make sure the other ships do, too. We'll do one pass. Take them off to Isallna, and I'll follow once my ship's repaired. I'll communicate our decision to Cathy on the way out."

"You sure you'll be all right here alone?" Arn raised an eyebrow.

"I'll be fine," Mira said. "Soporos is still running. Something else to thank Zekk for once his ego has deflated a good bit."

"So, never." Arn winked.

"I'll be there shortly," Daniel said. He ended his end of the call.

"Be safe," Arn said with a smile.

"Same to you," Mira said.

Arn ended the call.

Thirty minutes later, the Liberalis bridge lurched upwards, and the floor returned to a level orientation. Mira had spent the first five minutes after Arn and Daniel had left wondering if there would be some way for her to get Intersection Five residents into the Liberalis, but she didn't see any children asleep on the floor below her ship, and she wasn't confident in being able to haul a teenager or adult up through the airlock without injuring either them or herself, if she could even manage it at all. She had the rest of the Reconstructionists and the Isallnan Cooperatives depending on her, too. Try as she might, she could not devise a feasible plan to rescue anyone below, which made waiting all the more difficult. Mira found herself able merely to stare at *Behemoth*'s red cloth cover while she waited for the repairs to be complete. Every so often she gazed out into the blackness of the hangar bay and wondered at the pointlessness of this carnage. What had it all been for? So that a small group could continue to cling to their power and a large group could continue to struggle to gain a power they would never possess?

Eventually, Aurie's voice intoned over the Liberalis speakers. "Repairs are complete."

"Plot a course for Isallna," Mira said. "East Bremm Cooperative. Initiate metaxic engines when ready."

Moments later, the familiar hum filled the bridge, the blackness fizzled away into blue whorls, the helm control interface flickered into existence before her, and the Liberalis accelerated forward through the metaxia.

"Aurie, open a channel to Cathy Om." Mira braced herself in her chair. She was angry, but she needed to channel that anger. She needed to be fair, just. She needed to be the opposite of her foe, not out for blood, or revenge, or anything so vulgar as that. She needed to represent the force for good, and she didn't know if she was up to the task. Regardless, she would have to try.

"Mira?" Cathy's voice was all smiles.

"I've initiated a video call," Mira said.

"One moment." Cathy appeared before her, wearing her green and brown uniform, the one for the public. She had done herself up, particularly her hair, Mira noticed. And bright red lipstick, too. "How is the evacuation effort going?"

"It is done," Mira said. "For now."

Cathy's smile fell. "I don't understand. Only one group is underway—"

"I know what you did to Intersection Five. And Seventeen. And Forty-Two."

"I don't know what you—" Cathy was a good liar, but Mira was tired of it.

"And I know you illegally jailed Martin Venner. And I know you are holding a metaxic organism named Kalos hostage. And before you come after me, there are a great many other people who now know these things, too, and firing a Stolten bomb at Isallna won't get rid of them all. For example, there are all of the Reconstructionists, whom I'd like to remind you are very good at running."

Cathy's mouth was now a flat line. "We should talk more calmly about these things, Mira."

"I am quite calm. What I am here to tell you is that neither the Reconstructionists nor the Isallnan Cooperatives will be party to what you are doing here. We will not help ease the pain on your conscience by removing people from intersections you intend to destroy so that you can harvest their potentia in order to keep Intersection Thirteen stable."

Cathy's eyes flared and the flat line of her mouth became a scowl. "Then when they die, it will be on you."

Mira shook her head. "No. Because we will not push the button. The conditions for our help are simple. We will resume relocation efforts only when Kalos has been released, and when the government at Founder Square admits what it did to Intersections Five, Seventeen, and Forty-Two."

"We need that potentia much more than they do!" Cathy's eyes held fury. "Without Founder Square, there is no UMI."

"There never was a UMI, Cathy. You never had any society at all. You had a bunch of individuals who collected up stuff without knowing what any of it was worth in any measurement system other than potentia. That was why you had libraries filled with wonders that no one paid any attention to. Potentia isn't anything. It's literally nothing, just twisted up chunks of possibility that unravel with time. You can't make them real by holding a metaxic organism hostage, lying to people, or murdering them. That last decision will come back to haunt you very, very soon, unless the UMI leadership owns up."

204

"Is that a threat?"

"No. It is a statement of fact. The Reconstructionists have no desire for conflict, and neither does Isallna. But how many more times do you think you can blow up an 'inferior' Intersection before the remaining 'mediocrities' conclude that they are next in line?"

Cathy glared silently.

"The Isallnan Cooperatives and the Reconstructionists will be standing by on Isallna awaiting your reply."

"You won't be going back to Earth, then?"

"We won't be supplying you with an easy target for your weaponry, no."

"Is that all?"

"Yes." Mira let sadness into her voice. Had it been too hopeful to think that she might bring Cathy around? That she might be able to undo the societal conditioning to climb to the top of a hierarchy and hoard, hoard, hoard with every last fiber of one's being? "That is all," Mira added.

"Goodbye, then."

"Goodbye, Cathy."

Even into her teenage years, Mira's mother had overseen her education. They would sit together at the kitchen table and go over all of Mira's homework together. On one particular day when Mira was thirteen years old, it was a history lesson.

"The Hegemony was founded in 1945, shortly after the end of the Last Great War," Mira had said proudly.

"That is what is written in the book, yes." Her mother sat with her hands in her lap, her expression gaining that vaguely inquisitorial look that she often adopted when they read the history books.

"You keep saying that," Mira said. "If these books are filled with lies, then why should I bother reading them?"

"You need to know what the doctrine is, even if you one day come to question it, like your father and I have."

"What's the point, though? Why would our country print books filled with lies instead of the truth? It's annoying. What does it get them?" Mira threw herself back in her chair, adopting her pouty expression.

Her mother put her arms on the table and leaned toward her. "They get power. And from that comes money and status."

Mira bunched up her forehead. "I don't get why they can't just tell the truth. I just want real facts."

"Here's the thing, Mira. Even though we know that they're lies, we can't ever be certain about the truth. We think there was a country called the United States of America here for much longer than the Hegemony says, but we don't know how much longer or what happened to it. We think that something happened in 2020, but we don't know what. And the official line from the Hegemony is that nothing of importance occurred in 2020."

"How do we even know that much?"

"I can tell you when you're older."

"Why not now?" Mira was sitting up straighter now, and her tone was growing demanding.

Her mother stood up straighter in response. "Because they will hurt you."

Mira crossed her arms. "I wish someone would hurt them."

Her mother shook her head. "No, Mira. You must never wish that."

"Why not?"

"Because very little separates the person who injures and murders for money and power, from the person who injures and murders for a 'just' cause. Just causes have a way of becoming ambiguous, multifaceted, complex. No. That is not a good path. It can be justified to end a life, but it is very, very difficult to prove that out with moral certitude."

Mira was smart enough to know to keep her voice low for what she wanted to say next. "So, we really think it would bad if tomorrow all the Hegemony leaders were just gone?"

"Well," her mother smiled, "in that case, new, awful people would just fill the vacant posts and pick up where their predecessors had left off."

Mira deflated. "We can't do anything, then."

Her mother smiled. "We can. Every time we educate ourselves about how things really are. Every time we refuse to submit to injustice. Every time we help one another. Every time we say 'no' when it's proper and 'yes' when it's proper. When we treat others with compassion, but also with respect. Every time we uphold dignity and make vulgar, barbaric behavior a disgrace. Society is all of us, Mira. Every one of us has power over the world. We can choose our words and our actions. We can lash out, or we can bring people together. We make ourselves wise, or we can spew out ignorance and taint people's hearts. It's all up to us. I know how frustrating it is to tolerate the lies. But we must learn them, because in order to gain the time and space to become better people, we must pretend—most of the time—to be as ignorant, and therefore harmless, as all the rest."

"I hope one day I can just tell all those awful Hegemony goons what I think of them."

"Don't wish for that, Mira."

"Why not?"

"Wish instead that you can force them into better action. Into being good to others. That would be much better for everyone. Including yourself."

"I suppose."

"Anyway, that day is a long way off." Her mother smiled

again. "Now, again. Let's go over the lesson from the top. 1945."

Mira sighed and began again. "The Hegemony was founded in 1945, shortly after the end of the Last Great War." She then affected an air of smugness she had seen from characters on holodramas. "So it is written in the immaculate book my government has so graciously provided me." She added that with a smirk.

Her mother smirked back. "Keep going."

-11

The library at the University of East Bremm was a tall, impressive building. Another stone structure, but this one smaller than the central library. It contained a high-ceilinged room of shelves set into the walls with long desks spanning the interior and lights affixed at intervals. Above the walls were rows of stained glass windows, and since the longer walls faced east and west, it was a gorgeous place to read on a clear day in both the morning and the evening.

Mira, Arn, Enro, Trent, Enna, and Haden, all six pilots of the Reconstructionists' metaxic ships, sat in the library reading. They'd sent word back to Zekk on Earth, who was holding down their Granite Lake hideout along with Serra and Hanith. They had been instructed not to return any transmissions, for fear that that would allow the UMI to locate them.

Mira had finished *Behemoth* a few days prior, which her computer, having finally processed everything she'd scanned in the Intersection Thirteen Central Library, told her was more likely to have been titled *Leviathan* on Earth. Now she was reading Chaucer, having decided that she needed something a little more lighthearted overall, after all the recent excitement and intensity in her life.

The past twelve days had been uneventful on Isallna. Every day, an Isallnan patrol ship would fly out near the UMI, scan the media, return, and report. Five days after Mira had returned to Isallna, the patrol had reported that Intersections 1, 20, 26, and 34 had all experienced cataclysmic system failures, but the media had indicated that the populace had once again bought the line that this was due to negligence of local authorities in those Intersections. Five days after that, the patrols reported that Intersections 9 and 28 had also succumbed. This time there had been no report of public response one way or the other.

And then there was today—the day that Kalos had predicted Founder Square would lose power and he would be free.

Mira put down Chaucer and sat, looking up at the stained glass windows and the way the light hit the bookshelves on the other side of the wall. She wanted to see Zekk, Serra, and Hanith again, but being stuck on East Bremm was not so bad.

Arn nudged her and whispered, "You hear that?"

Mira listened carefully and heard voices, raised voices, just outside. Arn and Mira both stood and put down their books. Enro, Hanith, Enna, and Haden all soon followed suit. They hurried out the large double doors of the great room and down the half-circular stone staircase. Daniel came running up to them at its base, patrol pilots trailing in his wake, and he nodded for them to follow him away from the library.

"What's happened?" Mira asked once they'd started down the stone stairs in front of the library.

"Intersection Thirteen is collapsing," Daniel replied. "The other remaining intersections found the hangar bays of the destroyed intersections and shut down the gyrospires. Intersection Thirteen has lost over eighty percent of the potentia generation that was holding it together, and its rooms are collapsing much faster than they can evacuate people. Those who have gotten out are coming here."

"How many people are we talking?" Enna asked.

"Their total ship capacity when I was there was about a quarter-million people," Mira said. "That's if they jammed people in."

"They'll have done just that," Daniel said.

"What about other intersections?" Enro said. "They'll be evacuating now, too."

"Yes," Daniel said. "We should expect them as well. But we can only integrate so many here into our culture and way of life without destabilizing it. Fortunately, though, we've found some candidate worlds where refugees can start their own colonies. Hopefully, those groups will stick to actual universes this time."

Minutes later, they'd come to the field at the edge of the city of East Bremm where Mira and the other Reconstructionists had parked their metaxic ships.

Daniel looked at one of the patrol pilots.

"It will be any minute now," the pilot said.

Three large white vans with flashing red nanite lumens atop their roofs careened into view and parked themselves at the edge of the field. Just moments later, there was a great shimmering, at first just a few spots, and then more, dozens of them, filling the entire field.

Metaxic ships congealed into existence, appearing fuzzy at first, then gaining coherence. As soon as they were fully physical, hatches burst open and people began rushing out. Daniel and the Reconstructionists all jumped into action, searching out people who were wounded, and supporting them in reaching the ambulances, or, when necessary, bringing medical personnel to them.

Late that night, after things had settled down, Mira and the Reconstructionists sat in a meal hall having a late dinner. It was sparsely populated, since most had eaten earlier, and the whole group was exhausted.

"I suppose," Daniel intoned, after they'd finished eating, "you'll be heading back to Earth soon."

"We'll give it a few more days," Arn said. "Just to be sure. But yes."

"I understand you'll want to ensure the safety of your base on Earth," Daniel said, "but you're welcome back here any time."

"Thanks," Arn said. "The same goes for us. You can visit us anytime."

"I'd like that," Daniel said.

They said goodnight, and Mira, Arn, and the other Reconstructionists headed for the residence where they'd been staying. Mira very much had to remind herself that baths were a luxury she should not get too attached to.

Mira and Arm went to the room they shared and practically collapsed into their bed.

"How many days?" Mira asked.

"Oh, I don't know. Three or four. How about five, just to be on the safe side?"

"All those people…" Mira said. "Perhaps we shouldn't have given those stipulations."

"I think we made the right choice," Arn said, already closing his eyes and nestling his face into his pillow. "We would have been putting ourselves in terrible danger, and

212

they had every opportunity to receive our help. They just had to tell the truth. But they wanted to live out their delusion to the very end."

"I suppose." Mira relaxed into her pillow. "It'll be nice to have another week here. I just wish we could take this culture home with us. It's so weird not to have to be constantly worry about drones and soldiers and nanite surveillance and on and on—" Mira's eyes shot open. She jolted out of bed.

Arn's eyes fluttered open, and he pushed himself up with one arm. "What's wrong?"

"Nothing's wrong... I just had a thought. It was something my mother said once, and another detail that I remembered just now." Mira snatched up her computer out of her backpack and searched the net for a particular document.

"What are you looking for?" Arn asked.

"The Articles of Incorporation for an Isallnan Cooperative."

Arn squinted. "Why?"

Mira let out a small, triumphant laugh. "Wow. It just might work."

"What might work?"

"Do you know what the minimum number of people is that can form a cooperative?"

"No. What is it?"

"Nine."

"Then..."

"It's worked well enough for them. Maybe we can make it work for us."

-6

On their way back to Earth, the six Reconstructionists stopped their ships at a spot near where the UMI had been. They scanned the area, using programs they'd acquired from East Bremm, ones capable of detecting metaxically contorted spaces.

Mira, Arn, and the others each ran the scans from their respective ships, got on a shared call with one another, and aggregated the data. A kind of map appeared in front of Mira's monitor. There were scattered pieces of rooms, none of them connected. A few scraps of stable space here, badly intruded, a strip of space there—no single one of them big enough to contain anything except maybe some atmosphere, a spare pipe, crate, or some other such implement. The largest one they found was only about forty square meters, a tall room that had eroded around its periphery, probably the remains of Intersection Thirteen's gyrospire.

A calculation appeared at the bottom of the map: at the current rate of decay, the last bit of the UMI would disappear into the metaxia in just six days.

Arn opened a group call between all the ships.

"It's hard to tell exactly, but our Isallnan friends think around 300 million people weren't able to make it out in time. Those people won't get a proper commemoration, so I'd like us all to take a moment to reflect on what's happened here and remember those whose lives were needlessly lost."

Sad nods all around from the small rectangles superimposed over the viewport holding the image of the swirling blue of metaxic space. It was difficult for Mira to believe that this was the same place where she had stumbled upon a sprawling empire less than a month prior.

They closed out their group communication channel and the Reconstructionists' ships took off again toward Earth. Mira's thoughts turned to relief at finally being able to go home after so long, then promptly to the work that needed to start next.

She opened a private comm with Arn. "How are you doing?"

"Well enough. You?"

"Glad to be going home, finally."

"You've had quite an adventure out here. Good job on the literature, by the way. You were able to rescue a lot of it."

"It's sad how small that was compared to their total collection. I'd barely scratched the surface of Intersection Thirteen's books, let alone any of the others'."

"Every little bit helps. And this is more than a little."

"I suppose so." Mira tapped her fingers on the Liberalis console. "I wanted to ask about something else. Have you given any thought to my idea?"

"It's… I like it in theory. It's just such a long shot."

"It works for Isallna."

"But will it work for us?"

"I'm ready to make a stand, now that I've found a system worth fighting for."

"We still have to see what the others think."

"You're right. But those are good challenges to have. The only other option is to keep running, and I meant what I wrote to you the other day. I don't want to run anymore."

Acknowledgement

Although writing can be a lonely craft, it is untrue that writers operate in a vacuum. Each work benefits from the writer's accumulated experience. This novel is no different, but during its development, in particular, I benefited greatly from the support and advice of Michele Benchouk, Christopher Kulp, Aaron Ramos, and Serdar Yegulalp. As always, I am indebted to my husband, Alex, whose kind and attentive support knows no bounds.

As an independent writer and publisher, forming the interpersonal connections capable of reinforcing my creative energy is the hardest part by far. I am not exaggerating when I say that I could not have done it without you.